THE JUDAS SHI

BRIAN CALLISON was born in Manchester in 1934. He was educated at the High School of Dundee before entering the merchant navy in 1950 as midshipman with the Blue Funnel Line, sailing mainly on cargo liners to the Far East and Australia. On leaving the sea he studied at Dundee College of Art. He has held several administrative posts, including those of managing director of a construction company and general manager of a large entertainment centre.

He also served several years in the territorial army with the 51st Highland Division Provost Company, Royal Military Police, and now maintains an active connection with the sea as Head of Unit, Royal Naval Auxiliary Service.

His first phenomenally successful novel, *A Flock of Ships*, was published in 1970 and has already been translated into nine foreign languages. No less an authority than Alistair MacLean has said, 'there can be no better adventure writer in the country today.'

BRIAN CALLISON

The Judas Ship

FONTANA/Collins

First published by William Collins Sons & Co. Ltd 1978
First issued in Fontana Paperbacks 1979
Second impression May 1986

© Brian Callison 1978

Made and printed in Great Britain by
William Collins Sons & Co. Ltd, Glasgow

Part I

PROLOGUE

Sparks stared at me dully through a charred bacon-crisp expression of disbelief.

He was dead. I knew that much without even stepping across the coaming and into the gutted radio room. Even his tropical whites had incinerated under the explosive sear of the shell, yet strangely enough his epaulettes, still displaying the golden zig-zag rings of a chief radio operator, remained neat as a Swede schooner balanced on the scorched shoulders.

But blast can do that – leave some things precisely the way they were yet fragment everything else around into a smoking unrecognizable shambles. I'd seen it happen before, aboard the last ship they'd sunk under me, but for that matter quite a few merchant seamen like myself had learned a lot of new facts about the horror of war at sea over the past few months. It was a very good time for learning, was 1941.

For instance, by the end of that year a crewman aboard a torpedoed tanker might well have discovered that the main difference between a cargo of high octane and a cargo of fuel oil was that the gasoline ignited on the surface and cremated you from the outside inwards, while the furnace oil hardly ever managed to spark off at all, but went down your throat instead, right after it had blinded you, and burned your lungs into retching black sponges until you died. From the inside out.

Or imagine abandoning ship, leaping from the stern even while it's rising high into the air or letting yourself fall from the capsizing bridge deck before it rolls over on top of you. Now, you'll learn very quickly that you have two clear alternatives when going over the wall – either you wear a lifejacket, or you don't. So let's say you can't reach yours, or it's been taken by someone else, or you just opt for the fastest way off an' the hell with it, and jump without.

Well, firstly, there's a pretty fair chance you'll spit yourself on a floating spar. Or you might smash your skull against a jettisoned hatch board, or telescope yourself into the bows of the lifeboat which sheered frantically away from the falls forty feet below you at just the wrong moment . . . while even if you survive all that, you'll possibly still die because most sailors can't stay afloat without any kind of aid for very long, and a shiny black-oiled head in a shiny black-oiled sea is very hard to detect before shock and cramp and plain lethal hopelessness overcome you.

O.K.! So go with The Jacket, Flotation, Board of Trade recommended specification, and see what happens.

Well, firstly there's a pretty fair chance you'll spit yourself on a floating spar. Or you might smash your skull against a jettisoned hatch board, or telescope yourself . . ! But you learned all *that* already, a moment ago, when you watched what happened to Charlie after he'd abandoned without one. However you go anyway, seeing there's no real option, and you neatly miss all the spars and boards and boats . . .

. . . only to remember instead – when it's a screaming micro-second too late – that you've forgotten to clutch the front of your lifejacket hard down and against your chest as you hit the water. Which means it rises like a steam hammer as its buoyancy forces it under your chin, while your head snaps back in a neck-shattering arc to leave you just as dead as Charlie anyway.

6

Though certainly a sudden demise in that manner could save your learning about all the other snags which could spoil your day. Like the jacket presenting your dangling legs as a perfect target for shark and barracuda once the underwater rumblings from your sinking ship have reassuringly faded. Or the heat of a tropical sun which will drive you insane within hours. Or the cold of the Murmansk run which will kill you in twelve minutes flat, with or without that lifejacket of yours.

Or the wheeling, swooping seabirds. They peck and gouge with bomb-sight precision at a bloke in the water. So you die blind once again, just like it was the fuel oil that other time . . .

Mind you, that was only part of the new world of discovery. There were all sorts of other things a merchant seaman was likely to learn in the early nineteen forties from the new experiences contained in his war-at-sea syllabus.

For instance what might happen if you were sailing alone, as a fast independent, when the innocuous merchantman you'd sighted a little while earlier suddenly altered sharply towards you, ran up a German Naval Ensign in place of the neutral flag she'd flown until that moment, and ordered you not to use your radio or you would be fired upon.

Only you did just that anyway – because the Admiralty had told you that was what you had to do – and transmitted the frantic warning prefix RRRR, followed by your war call sign and text:

. . . GBXJ . . . M.V. MAYA STAR . . . AM BEING CHALLENGED BY SURFACE RAIDER IN POSITION . . .

. . . Well, you'd soon discover that you probably wouldn't be able to complete that vital call for help, because you'd already have used up all the time that anonymous warship out there needed to read your transmission, open fire on your upperworks and radio room, and smear your chief operator into a charred, vaguely incredulous object-lesson on the effects of heat and blast.

7

Which meant it had all started again, the learning part, as I stood there desperately trying to remember where I'd left my bloody lifejacket and trying, at the same time, to make that decision as to whether I'd be better off with, or without, it.

Until, from the forr'ad end of the boat deck, another shell exploded deafeningly. Square on the bridge.

I

It had all seemed to happen so quickly.

Seven in the morning. A grey, irritable day with visibility clamping down to around three miles and the sullen Atlantic swell beginning to crumble into smaller, more vicious lumps of white-crowned water. But it could get like that sometimes, even off the Brazilian coast. In fact if it hadn't been for the equatorial heat, that humid, debilitating miasma carrying the smell of rotting jungle vegetation two hundred miles out to sea, we might easily have been punching across the North Atlantic instead of heading sou' easterly on a six thousand-odd mile run to the bottom of Africa.

As Chief Officer I had the four to eight watch along with the Fourth Mate and young Davidson, our senior apprentice. Quartermaster Tennison straddled the wheel to make up the morning quartet wearing, as usual, his recently acquired and somewhat reproachful expression which always made me feel a little uncomfortable. As if I'd forgotten to do something, somehow. Like be nice to him.

Down aft, along the boat deck, the day work crowd were turned-to with deck scrubbers under the earthy direction of Bosun Fletcher, personally controlling the hose with all the expertise of a professional fireman. Someone was wistfully harmonizing along with the laborious metre of bristle on plank about how there was goin' ter be blue skies oooover the white cliffs o' Doooover . . .

Sometime. After the bloody war ended!

Further aft, right on the poop, I could see the D.E.M.S. guncrew sponging out the barrel of the *Maya Star*'s main, and for that matter only, armament. A 4.5-inch naval gun which either fired its thirty pound shell from the centre of a hanging cloud of rust dust, cordite smoke and displaced paint particles – or didn't fire at all. And when that happened a nervous Bombardier Timmer, looking for all the world like a fish out of water – which he was in a sense, only the other way round seeing he was a soldier aboard a ship on a posting from the army's new Maritime Regiment – well, Timmer had to clear the poop, open the breech before a sea of hushed, expectant faces watching from every blast-protected part of the ship, and gingerly drop the extracted misfire over the side.

We all clapped then. In fact the first time he did it we were so noisily spontaneous and anticipatory that Timmer thought the bloody shell had gone off in his arms and dropped it on the deck instead. Which halted the applause instantly. The Bombardier reckoned later that it had halted his heart-beat for about four minutes as well but I thought he was being over-modest. I didn't think he'd stayed petrified as a deep-frozen ballet dancer for more than three at the outside.

Everything else about the ship was reassuringly normal. The exhaust from the funnel puttering and roaring a healthy diesel-blue haze above us as the rim of the funnel itself scribed lazy elliptical arcs against the overcast sky. Hatch-locking bars glinting in neat parallel lines down the foredeck while an occasional curl of spray whipped inboard over the bows to spatter hissingly across the fo'c'slehead. The Carpenter, wearing a sickly yellow sweat shirt bought in New York, moving methodically along the forward well deck with junior apprentice Meehan in tow, checking all hatch wedges secure.

Routine. Almost like it had been in the old days, before the war. Only now there are differences, and not only because we had an alien *Prima Donna* of a gun mounted on our specially reinforced poop.

Everything was grey now, for a start. Grey hull, grey upperworks, grey funnel, grey ventilators and rails and winches and doors and lifeboats and . . . God but it was a grey world, this wartime environment. Grey and soulless, like the face of a drowned sailorman.

There was protective concrete on the bridge too, now, where originally there had been the warm glow of varnished teak and well-scrubbed canvas dodgers. And there were sandbags round the wheelhouse windows, and steel plates with roughly acetylened edges to snatch at your clothes in the middle of the night.

There were extra Carley floats in case we were torpedoed. And extra fire points in case we were bombed. Extra shaded stern lights in case we were in convoy, and extra distress flares in case we weren't.

Even the gleaming brass binnacle on the monkey island above me had been painted. Battleship bloody grey, of course!

And then the Old Man climbed the starboard ladder to the bridge.

It was three minutes past seven in the morning watch. December. 1941 . . .

And all that had been less than fourteen minutes ago.

That's all it had taken them to surprise and outmanoeuvre us. I knew that much because the fickleness of the first explosion had left the radio room clock secured to the bulkhead above the operator's desk. Betty Grable still looked in pretty good shape too, with only one corner of her photograph burned away, but they'd decapitated Deanna Durbin with a scalpel-clean shrapnel slash right across her exquisite hair line.

The main transmitter had been obliterated. There wasn't anything there any longer other than a jagged gap in the starboard side through which I could see a ventilator eyeing me vacantly from the boat deck. There was a hole through the ventilator as well. More or less the same diameter as the one I was staring through.

The emergency transmitter looked like the guts of a robot opened for inspection. The front of the casing was sheared off cleanly to expose a stiffly erect tableau of valves, condensers and a souvenir metal casting of the Empire State Building which had somehow been deposited there on the shock wave.

A second round erupted from the direction of the bridge, the whole ship shuddering with the impact of it.

I heard myself squeal 'Oh *Christ* . . !' in terror while Sparks slowly slipped out of the operator's chair and sort of collapsed on deck. His right arm, black and dehydrated, remained vertical, fused to the transmitter key. I began to back away, unable to tear my eyes from the charnel house of the *Maya Star*'s radio room, until a terrifying splutter of incandescence showered across the deck and the Empire State Building began to melt as it shorted out the H.T. leads of the transmitter.

And then something clutched my shoulder. Convulsively.

I yelped with the shock of it, whirling round and stepping back as a wild figure barged past me across the coaming, then stopped. Dead! Before uttering a muffled, retching sob.

I said, 'He's finished, Martin. The whole bloody ship's going to be finished . . .'

The Second Operator stared at me. I could see the tears trickling down his soft cheeks, glistening among the long dark lashes that had done so much for the ladies of Charleston, South Carolina, while we were loading outward.

'I jus' nipped along to the heads. It should've been me in that chair only he told me to take a break, he'd listen-in till breakfast . . .'

The ship rolled uneasily, except that the deck stayed canted fractionally to starboard and I knew we were altering course, turning steadily to port and away from the raider. Then I remembered the detonations from the bridge and felt a sickening foreboding that we weren't under the control of human agency any longer, that now the *Maya Star* was simply a rogue ship, running blind as the eyes of a cadaver helmsman.

The Old Man. The Fourth Mate . . . the Davidson kid. Dolefully reproachful Tennison . . . God only knew what expression of disapproval the quartermaster must have been wearing as that first shell impacted beside him, knowing I wasn't even there when it happened despite the fact that it had been my watch on the bridge.

'He said he couldn't sleep,' Sparks whispered doggedly, while the shorting wires in the cabin *crick-cracked* and flashed like sprays of blue tumbling stars. 'Go an' grab a coffee, son. I'll listen-in till breakfa . . .'

Suddenly, involuntarily, I tensed.

There was something there, under my feet. For a numbed few seconds I didn't know what it was, what could be happening to hone the fear in me to an even finer edge . . . until I realized it wasn't something new, that it had been there all the time, ever since we'd left the States – it was the vibration.

And that meant we were still steaming at full speed! That they still couldn't know what the hell was happening below in the engine room. And that, presumably, there wasn't anyone left on the bridge to tell them . . .

Swinging Sparks against the bulkhead I snatched a fire extinguisher from its rack, slamming it violently into his arms. 'Do *something*!' I snarled, fighting the rising hysteria in me. 'Put the bloody fire out, laddie, 'cause I've got to GO . . .'

And then I was running. Charging dementedly towards the door to the boat deck and the remains of the bridge, with the apprehension building to a tight, agonized ball inside me.

I had to STOP her! Get word to the engineers on watch before that disguised warship out there mistook our erratic alteration of course as a determination to run for it.

Because I'd already guessed that she was a fully-operational German surface raider. That she probably mounted at least six 5.9-inch guns as well as maybe two or four torpedo tubes – and that she was now cruising just over one thousand yards off our starboard beam.

While I knew all *we* had was the one solitary, antiquated stern chaser with all the hitting power of a catapult. And even *that* didn't always manage to go off when Bombardier Timmer squeezed the bloody trigger.

It had been odd, really. Almost as if the Old Man had had some sort of a premonition as he'd reached the head of the bridge ladder a little earlier.

He'd simply halted, glancing astern bleakly instead of making his usual first move towards the wheelhouse and compass, checking to ensure that the course steered precisely matched the chalked figures on the helmsman's course board and, incidentally, infuriating me beyond measure at the same time.

Whereupon he'd invariably growl, 'Watch her head, Quartermaster!', entirely irrespective of whether the magnetic card was five degrees off or splitting the lubber's line right down the middle – and *that* routine warning always got the duty helmsman purple-faced with barely controlled and self-righteous indignation.

He was a good captain, Jeremy Prethero. A nice man who loved his ship and looked after his crew. But my God he was an irritable old woman first thing in the morning watch!

Anyway, today had been different. A break with accepted tradition. Instead he'd simply stayed where he was, gripping the sanded teak rail and facing aft, eyes fixed disapprovingly on the figures busy around our gun. Even after I'd moved up behind him and said, 'Good morning, Sir,' he hadn't answered. Not for a minute.

Then he'd snorted loudly. 'They'd no right,' he'd muttered. 'No right at all to put that damned thing aboard us. It's provocative, that's all it is. Provocative an' damned useless.'

I'd followed his eyes, wondering absently whether he meant the gun or Bombardier Timmer. 'It's only defensive,'

I offered placatingly. 'We aren't expected to attack anyone with it.'

The Old Man looked at me scathingly and I thought, 'Oh *hell*, he's going to be bloody-minded all day.' 'It's still a provocation, Mister. Soon as we make a move to man that, even in defence, Jerrie can use it as an excuse to claim we've performed a warlike act and sink us out of hand.'

'They'll do that anyway, soon as we use our wireless. The Germans have always argued that radio transmissions offer resistance to capture. They consider themselves justified in opening fire as soon as we go on the air.'

'Aye? Well that's different!' the captain growled dogmatically. I could have sworn he turned slightly at the same time, making sure I noticed the four rings on his epaulette inferring that his argument won on the grounds of seniority. 'Come to that, Mister Barton, the British Navy claims that even sailing merchantmen in escorted convoys offers resistance – d'you reckon we should all steam on our own wi'out any protection because've that, then?'

'But we *are* on our own,' I pointed out diffidently, feeling, at the same time, that somehow the point of the discussion had got a bit mixed up. 'And anyway, it's not the Royal Navy's attitude I'm worried about.'

'That's precisely what I *mean*,' the Old Man retorted, victoriously if a little obscurely.

'Yessir,' I acknowledged. Diplomatically.

Then we'd both leaned on the rail watching the activity below while the ship throbbed easily in a slow, spiralling motion under the low sky, and the only splash of colour was in the flap of the Red Ensign against the ruler-straight wake disappearing finally into the grey overcast astern.

'Get yer brush in them scuppers,' the Bosun yelled, putting on a special show for our benefit. 'You stop standin' round like you was part of the cargo, Ernie Tolliver an' Cleese, an' get scrubbin' *jaldi*!'

The Second Operator, Martin, stepped out of the radio room and edged his way past the splash of the hose towards

15

the entrance to the officers' quarters. He saw us watching and grinned cheerfully before disappearing. The Old Man grunted.

'Likes girls too much, that one. Mrs Prethero would've been horrified if she'd seen the way he carried on back in the States. Horrified.'

I grinned inwardly. Mrs Prethero was horrified at most things which, on reflection, probably accounted for the captain's bloody-mindedness first thing in the mornings.

'He's a good lad, Martin. Conscientious.'

On the poop Bombardier Timmer swung himself smoothly down from where he'd been cleaning astride the gun barrel – and stepped neatly into a bucket of water. A peal of laughter drifted forward to the bridge.

'Mrs Prethero would be horrified if she knew we had a gun on board,' the Old Man pondered morosely.

'*Scrub*, Ricketts!' the Bosun roared. 'Stop buggerin' about an' bloody SCRUB!'

Routine. The chunk of mallet on wood from forward as Chippie firmed the wedges; the whisper of the sea along our dipping flanks; the smell of breakfast beginning to drift upwards from the galley and through the midships accommodation where most of our complement still slept.

A Brazilian seagull side-slipped in and landed on the engine room skylight, watching us curiously through beady, shining eyes. I glanced surreptitiously at my watch, wondering how long it would be before the captain finally did remember to check on our course steered, and how much more petulant Quartermaster Tennison's expression must be growing under the tension of anticipation.

Routine. In a grey but still homely world. The sort of world I'd known for over twenty years, ever since signing as a wide-eyed kid of fifteen, outward bound for Valparaiso in a stick-funnelled old coal burner which corkscrewed and rolled every last retch of home- and sea-sickness out of my system – and kindled in me a love of ships and a respect for the sea which still diminishes only a little when the Atlantic

16

snow whips horizontally across the bridge at three o'clock in the morning, or the wind strength rises to a screech of hatred so that you can do little other than stare bleakly up at the breaking crests rearing high above your head and wonder – just for a few doubtful moments – if that chum you had at school, the one who left to be a bricklayer, might not have had a little more sense than you gave him credit for.

Two decades with the one mistress. Oh, I'd married once, but it hadn't lasted longer than three voyages. She hadn't accepted the prospect of an almost permanent single bed and a husband whose presence was felt for ninety-five per cent of the time by watching her stiffly from a Woolworth's photograph frame. So we parted. Or she ran away, actually, with a cashier from the bank down the road, and I still can't help smiling a little when I think about it. They put him in prison for fraud a few months later – so June still has a lonely bed, and a lover watching even more petulantly from that same Woolworth's frame. Or maybe there's another banker by now, while you can always turn a photograph to face the wall.

Twenty-odd years. From steam and coal dust to diesel engines, from apprentice aboard a clapped-out tramp to chief officer of one of the Company's newest and fastest cargo-liners. I'd learned a lot, but as I've already said, now I was learning a lot more as the spectre of Hitler's *Kriegsmarine* lurked just beyond the horizon. A thirty-six-year-old sailorman still assimilating the basic crafts of survival at sea, because now they were the arts of mistrust and suspicion, of when to run from a threat before it materialized ... even to run from the *threat* of a bloody threat ...

'SCRUB!' yelled the Bosun.

'Horrified, she'd be,' brooded the Old Man distantly, presumably still reflecting on the tight-lipped disapproval Mrs Prethero afforded to most things and most people.

And that was the moment when – without any warning – the war suddenly caught up with the *Maya Star*.

Or at least the fear of it did. At first.

'Ship, Sir . . . forr'ad of the port beam!'

The Old Man and I whirled in company while Gulliver, the Fourth Mate, was already on his way through the wheelhouse to the port wing where Davidson stood pointing.

'Whereaway?'

'There, Sir. About two points forward of the beam. Just a shape . . .'

I sprinted after them, grabbing for the spare binoculars on my way while, behind me, the Old Man came as far as the port door and stopped.

'You sure, lad?'

The boy didn't turn round. 'Yessir. I saw something, but it's gone now.'

'How's your heading, Quartermaster?'

Tennison's reply was defensive as ever. 'Sou' east by east, Cap'n. *Exactly!*'

'Starboard the wheel. Steer sou' sou' east.'

'Steer sou' sou' east, Sir . . .'

Tennison spun the wheel and we began to turn slowly, away from whatever it was that young Davidson had seen. I caught a glimpse of the apprentice's face just then, still straining to pierce the murk on our port side, and caught a hint of pleasure mingling with the tension. I knew it meant something to him, having his report acted on without doubt or question, and my heart warmed to little Jeremy Prethero who had the ability to know when to stop being a mistrusting old woman.

Mrs Prethero would've been horrified though. At her husband's faith in the word of a mere eighteen-year-old boy.

He hurried out and stood beside us, four pairs of eyes probing the haze-restricted horizon. 'Just in case,' the captain muttered defiantly. 'Damn the war.'

The swing of our head slowing now. A lumpy sea

disintegrated under the bow, spattering the foc'slehead while Chippie hesitated beside number one hatch, head raised interrogatively, feeling the course alteration under his feet.

'Steady on south sou' east, Sir.'

'Aye, aye. Steady as you go.'

All of us peering abaft the beam, making allowance for our own change of track. 'I *did* see something, Sir,' the apprentice said emphatically, a little anxiously.

Silence. Apart from the sigh of the water and the steady purr of our funnel exhaust. Even the sounds of activity from the boat deck party had halted temporarily, sensing that something was happening.

The seagull from Brazil preened itself luxuriously . . .

'*There!* Broad on the quarter . . . a ship.'

Three pairs of binoculars slammed simultaneously under three furrowed brows. The boy Davidson just shaded his eyes, there weren't enough glasses to go around aboard the *Maya Star*. I caressed the knurled ring of the Barr and Strouds and the darker break in the overcast sprang into focus.

Until . . .

'She's a merchantman!' I breathed, the initial wave of relief swamping over me. 'Not a warship.'

Though not everybody was as pleased as me.

'She could still be an armed raider, Sir,' the Fourth Mate suggested tentatively. 'Either the *Kormoran* or the *Atlantis* were reckoned to have hunted this area earlier on.'

The anonymous vessel began to assume a third dimension as she came on, still holding course to pass astern of us on a sou' westerly heading. She was steaming fast and already I could make out details of boats and ventilators surmounted by a low, slightly raked funnel. A modern diesel ship like ourselves, probably built around thirty-eight or -nine.

'There haven't been any enemy sighting reports from these waters for three months past,' the Old Man speculated, still gripping his glasses with unwavering concentration.

'She's still wearing her funnel livery, Mister. Can you make it out?'

'Yellow all the way to the top. There's a motif in red . . . initials of some sort.'

'Gdynia-Amerika Line?' Gulliver offered.

'Don't guess, Mister Gulliver. And they probably ceased operating soon as Jerrie invaded Poland anyway.'

'Aye,' I muttered dryly. 'They're probably all converted to the German flag now. As commerce raiders!'

Still closing fast but shaping to cut through our wake maybe half a mile astern. I began to feel easier as the seconds passed but that was the trouble with this bloody war, once upon a time you looked forward to meeting other ships as a break in the watch-keeping monotony. Now you immediately shrank away from the fear of the unknown, trying to hide in a blacked-out world of secrecy or at least keeping your stern presented to the stranger with speed as your greatest ally.

Our new world. Our new, grey, nervously furtive world.

'Break out the Aldis, Mister Gulliver,' the Old Man snapped. 'Ask her "What ship?".'

She answered right away. They'd probably been watching us as anxiously as we them. 'M.V. MONTE TEIDE . . .' the Fourth Mate read laboriously, '. . . CIA NAV SOTA AZ . . .'

'I c'n see her ensign, Sir,' Davidson blurted, pleased as a dog with two tails at being first. 'She's Spanish.'

Even the captain grinned with relief. 'Naviera Aznar Company out of Bilbao. It makes sense all right.'

I smiled back. A little weakly. 'Our original course?'

'Aye, we're wasting fuel and the Chief won't be happy about that.'

Prethero gestured to the Fourth Mate. 'Send our own name and wish her *bon voyage*, Mister.'

I continued to watch the crossing stranger, now almost directly astern of us, for a moment longer, then turned to our lugubrious helmsman. 'Come port again to sou' east by east . . .'

The captain winked at me slyly, and added, '. . . *exactly*, Quartermaster Tennison. *If* you please!'

Ten minutes ago. It seemed unbelievable. Only ten minutes ago, with the scare dying away and Jeremy Prethero suddenly in high good humour, smiling with his eyes crinkled and bright and the fuzzy white hair sticking sideways from under the gold-braided cap.

Only ten minutes ago.

Yet now . . .

I raced round the corner of the deck housing, on to the run of the boat deck itself, and then slowed abruptly while glancing wildly around with the hysteria rising within me like a lost child who didn't know what to do.

The bodies, first . . . apparently nothing but bodies of men strewn in contorted, rag-doll attitudes. Then the boats . . . both starboard boats holed by splinters with number one now hanging vertically from one davit, secured only by the after fall. And smoke creeping up behind me from the radio room. *God* . . . more smoke billowing heavily, ominously, from the doors to the crew accommodation. The Bosun's fire hose snaking and writhing like some living creature where it had been abandoned, the wallowing jet smashing debris and shattered glass and bright red blood into the scuppers and over, down to the rushing sea fifty feet below.

An' the bridge . . .?

'CHRIST!'

I accelerated again to a crazy headlong gallop, leaping clear over a thing with a deck scrubber still clutched in its hand but no head to its shoulders . . .

'Provocation' the captain had called it – that gun mounted at our stern. Yet they'd done all *this* to us before we'd even fired a shot. Because we'd simply tried to send a radio message . . . a cry for help.

But still only a minimum of force, they could claim. Merely a restrained warning confined to our bridge and W.T. cabin. And it simply couldn't be helped if a few things got damaged which happened to be sited in between. Like most of the *Maya Star*'s off-watch and sleeping crewmen . . .

I felt the anger rising again as I panted across that killing ground. Just as it had done a few minutes ago. When they'd first stopped me having a shave . . .

I remember standing out there on the bridge wing after the Old Man had impishly trailed off into the wheelhouse to plague the gloomy Tennison a little more. I'd still been watching the Spaniard absently, thinking how pleasant it must be for a neutral and wondering what kind of cargo they could be shipping in those long packing cases on deck. Certainly nothing warlike – machinery probably, or tractors bound for Paramaribo.

Gulliver hesitated beside me, coiling the lead of the Aldis in his hand. 'You were second mate on the *Inca Star* weren't you, Sir? When she was torpedoed?'

I nodded shortly. And thought about the oil on the water again, and the grilling heat from the sun. And the barracuda, and those bloody horrific little crabs. About the heads lolling on shattered spines above semi-submerged life-jackets . . . and about Charlie. Especially about Charlie.

Remember him? He was the chap who'd jumped on to the end of a vertically floating spar . . . and he'd been our fourth mate, just like Gulliver. He'd lived for three whole days after that. It had taken us nearly two of them simply to saw the projecting stump off short with a sheath knife . . .

'What was it like?'

I shrugged. 'It wasn't nice. Not really . . .'

Then I noticed the seagull watching me still from the engine room skylight and shivered involuntarily. They looked so different, so unutterably evil when those hooked razor beaks were on a level with your own eyes as you floated helplessly in a glassy sea.

Hurriedly I shifted my gaze, back to the yellow-funnelled *Monte Teide* now heading out of our wake and off to starboard. It was odd, in a way. For some reason she looked smaller than I'd first imagined, shorter somehow, yet her bow wave seemed bigger, as if she'd put on speed.

'No dog-legs in our course mind, Quartermaster Tennison.' Jeremy Prethero's jocular and no doubt unappreciated little quip from the wheelhouse.

'Get SCRUBBIN' then, you lot, an' stop standin' like you wus on yer daddy's yacht!'

Which was Bosun Fletcher's completely un-jocular quip from the boat deck.

Chunk . . . chunk . . . The Carpenter's measured mallet tap from the foredeck . . . I ran my hand pensively around my chin then stretched luxuriously, feeling the fatigue of the four to eight draining away under the promising aroma of American canned bacon for breakfast.

'Think I'll nip below while the Old Man's here, Four Oh. Have a shave an' a . . .'

Then I froze. Completely. In mid-stretch, like a crucified man with a yawn on his face.

Because the Spanish *Monte Teide* was steadily shrinking even more. That space between her masts *was* getting smaller and smaller and smaller . . .

Until I realized that it really wasn't anything like that at all. That the other vessel was simply turning sharply towards us on a parallel and, in view of her increased speed, an overtaking course to bring her maybe half a mile off our starboard side.

Which was the moment when the fear came back and the first certainty of impending disaster. And yet another pearl of wisdom to add to my book of learning about war at sea – namely that, when you do decide to run, then keep on running! Don't let them close that critical few miles gap between your stern and their guns, no matter what flag they pretend to be sailing under.

So I just kept my arms outstretched and began waving

23

them wildly instead, while bellowing in outraged fury, 'Bastards! The bastards've conned us all the way down the line . . .'

Before barging past a stunned Fourth Mate Gulliver, sprinting into the wheelhouse, clawing an equally dazed apprentice out of the way and snatching the engine telegraphs to 'Stand-by'.

The Old Man's voice snapped, 'What in the name o' God are you doing, Mister Barton?' and I looked up to see both Prethero and Tennison eyeing me blankly, perhaps a little nervously, though our doleful helmsman had managed to inject a trace of I-told-you-so reproach in *his* particular stare even then.

'She's a phoney,' I snarled. 'She's as Spanish as sauer-kraut an' lederhosen. *And* she's steaming like the clappers up our ass!'

He was very quick to catch up, Jeremy Prethero. He simply fell over the coaming to the bridge wing, took one tight glance astern then whirled towards Gulliver. 'She's calling us too, dammit. Read and report, man . . . Mister Barton!'

'Sir.'

'Work up our position.'

'What about the gun?'

'*Damn* the gun, Mister! Just calculate our position . . . Son.'

'Yessir?' An excited squeak. The boy's eyes were like organ stops and bright as a . . . a seagull's.

'Telephone the radio room. Tell them to stand-by to send a surface raider warning. Quickly now!'

Gulliver's barely controlled voice from the wing. 'Message reads . . . STOP . . . YOUR . . . SHIP . . . DO . . . NOT . . .'

I tried to stop my hand shaking as I snatched for the brass dividers, fumbling to lay off our distance run from my 0600 dead reckoning position. The pencil point broke as I marked the cross indicating our current whereabouts and I blurted a panicky '*Damn*!', scrabbling for a replacement. My hand left a crinkled, sweat-soaked patch on the signal pad as I scribbled our latitude, placing us some two hundred miles off São Luis do Maranhao with the mouth of the Amazon our starboard quarter.

The dividers skidded into place to tally longitude and I scrawled that too, and was on my way back into the wheel-house before Gulliver had finished reading the distant lamp.

'... REPEAT ... DO NOT USE YOUR WIRELESS OR ...'

I didn't listen to the 'Or'. I didn't need to. Because through the open door I could see that the *Monte Teide* – which certainly wasn't the real *Monte Teide* by now – wasn't even Spanish any longer. Not since she'd struck her flag at the stern and broken out another one instead, a much larger one, above the bridge.

The new one was blood red and black with just a touch of white. Actually it looked very impressive – the Ensign of the German *Kriegsmarine*.

It also meant that, from this moment on, they could sink us any time they wanted to, and quite legally. Within the terms of the Geneva Convention, of course ... or according to Hitler's interpretation of it anyway.

And that was the moment when a very odd thing happened.

'C'n I 'ave my lifejacket from over there, Mister Barton,' Tennison asked.

Not that the request was strange, not under the circumstances. But it was the way he'd made it – in such a satisfied almost pleased sort of voice.

I passed him the jacket, eyeing him numbly. He slipped it over his head, then saw me watching and smiled faintly, a little apologetically. 'I feel better now. A lot more settled, like,' he explained. 'I been worried y'see, Mister Barton. Some'ow I knew we wus doomed ... ever since we left the

States I knew we wus doomed, an' now I feels better. Knowin' *how*, if y'see what I mean?'

I swallowed. It all seemed so logical – knowing Tennison. 'I'm happy that you're happy . . .' I muttered ridiculously. And half wondered if it would really make his day if they managed to blow him to pieces.

And then I forgot about Tennison's macabre reassurance. In fact I forgot about pretty well everything for a moment of utter disbelief, when a distant, totally unexpected roar carried from aft.

'Take post . . . ! Prepare to enGAGE hostile bearing wun thuree zero . . .'

'Oh *Christ* . . .' I heard myself mutter. Rather weakly.

It would have been laughable. In any other situation but the one we were in.

'He's mad!' the Old Man's voice spluttered faintly. 'I never ordered them to . . .'

Then he rushed furiously to the after rail and leaned over, shaking his fist. 'You on the *gun* . .. BELAY that!'

'Fuse for impact.'

'Leave that bloody gun ALONE, man . . . !'

'Fuse . . . *set!*'

'Load one round . . .'

The captain came charging back into the wheelhouse purple with rage. 'You get *down* there, Mister! Tell 'em to get away from that damn weapon. Clear the poop altogether.'

'Yessir.' I held the signal pad out to him. 'Our position. D'you really intend to transmit, though. After their warning?'

'I do, Mister Barton. In my opinion it does not constitute a warlike act.'

'Oh God,' I thought bleakly. It was more the opinion of that other captain out there which worried *me* . . . but we'd been all through this before and Mrs Prethero would have been horrified if I'd wasted any more time arguing with her husband at such a critical moment.

'The engines then?' I prompted nervously. 'I've only rung them on to stand-by . . .'

The Prethero tone was like a razor slash as he reached for the radio room telephone. 'Get *aft*, dammit! I shall heave-to when I am assured that the proper procedures have been followed . . . but I will *not* provoke them any further by aggressive action with that stupid weapon. D'you hear me, Mister?'

I heard myself retorting 'Aye, aye,' in a hopeless growl, then I was on my way down the ladder and pushing through the crowd clustered uneasily around the still-jetting hose. Fletcher was eyeing the overtaking ship with a very bleak expression which didn't soften one bit as he diverted it to me.

'Get 'em over to the port boats quickly, Bose,' I threw as I passed. 'Get as much protection as you can behind the housing.'

It was only an ineffectual gesture – and I knew it wouldn't help those men already in the accommodation – but there wasn't time for anything else, not if I was to try to stop Bombardier Timmer's suicidal gesture from actually taking place.

And I was right, too. About the time.

In fact, I'd only managed to get as far as the bottom of the after well deck ladder when the first incoming shell hit the *Maya Star* . . .

I don't know whether I could have changed anything, even if I had managed to reach the poop gun in time.

Either way I never did. As soon as I heard, and felt, that initial detonation almost directly above me I . . . well . . . I forgot momentarily about our own gunners and the order Jeremy Prethero had given me to prevent them retaliating, and frantically scrambled all the way back up to the radio room instead . . .

. . . to find our chief operator already staring blindly at me

27

through that burned, faintly disbelieving mask while the next two 'cautionary' shells landed on our bridge.

And I'd known instantly that Sparks had died for nothing. Not for one damned shred of advantage. His fixed expression in itself told me he couldn't possibly have completed any four-R call – the surface raider alert – because they hadn't even allowed him enough time to understand what was happening himself.

While now I had another priority task ahead of me – to stop this runaway monster before the raider mistook our headlong rush as a determination to escape and continued the slaughter, venting a full salvo next time which would batter us into an exploding, sinking shambles within a few minutes . . .

I'd almost reached the buckled bridge ladder when I heard yet another cracking, flat report from astern. Sickly I skidded to a second involuntary halt, whirling to see what else Jerrie had discovered to shoot at down aft.

Just before blurting a heart-felt groan of utter despair as I realized that they hadn't hit *anything* during the past few moments, that the raider had still held her fire with Teutonic self-control despite our uncertain intentions, and that – instead – the situation had chillingly reversed itself.

Because Bombardier Timmer and the rest of our pathetic little gun's crew had just fired *back*, f'r God's sake!

And in a very provocative manner indeed.

2

Slam!

'Relooooooad . . ! FIRE!'

Slam!

'REload . . . ! Up twenty. On . . . on . . . ON . . . !'

That *bloody* gun on our poop! And Timmer. *And* the rest of those ridiculous optimists now working frenziedly around the platform as the brassy gleam of ammunition passed smoothly from the ready-use locker to the clanging breech . . . three figures stripped to the waist above khaki denim trousers marked our gallant but accident-prone Bombardier and his other two army oppo's, while an outrageous assortment of sartorial informality ranging from seaboots under bathing trunks to a steward's white mess jacket crowned by a bowler hat, picked out the rest of the gun's crew drawn from the *Maya Star*'s own complement.

I roared un-nautically, 'Cut it OUT! Leave the bloody thing *ALONE* . . .'

The gunlayer's arms working like pistons as he swept the long barrel, following the raider's track. '. . . On TARGET.'

'FIIIIIRE!'

Slam . . . ! The projectile leaving the gaping muzzle, ripping through belching cordite gasses with the fading screech of a departing banshee.

'Reloaaaad . . . an' keep that ammo *movin*' there!'

I opened my mouth to shout again, convulsively squeezing the already tortured ladder rail at the same time . . .

. . . until – suddenly – there was a brief spurt of flame right against the after end of the other ship, followed by a steadily increasing plume of black oily smoke which tumbled down over her counter and lay like a thick, pulsating carpet along her wake.

And I just stared disbelievingly, already dumbfounded by the realization that Timmer had managed even to *fire* the venerable weapon, never mind hit something with it as well, while somebody in the gun's crew began bawling with enormous excitement, 'We *hittem!* Oh, we laid one on they bastids right in the . . .'

But that was the moment when the fear came back to me. And the hopelessness.

For I could still see the raider framed neatly in the space left between the inverted bow of number three boat and the bulk of the suspended, slowly-pirouetting number one . . . and even as I watched the enemy ship seemed to sparkle all along her length while a new cloud of lighter grey smoke drifted rapidly astern on the wind of her passage.

I'd suddenly understood what really had been concealed under those packing cases on her decks just as the scream of the incoming salvo stopped dead – and the *Maya Star* felt as though she was lifting clear out of the water on a crescendo of rippling detonation.

Until something as unyielding as a steel bulkhead moved over and slammed into me. I was thrown violently to one side, whirled around with my mouth wide and sucking as if in a vacuum, then blown helter-skelter along a million miles of deck before ending on my back, spread-eagled and frowning blankly up at the grey sky.

It gradually occurred to me that the decapitated man I'd leapt over a moment ago – the chap with a broom still clutched in one hand – must've been Ordinary Seaman Tolliver, Ernie, because now he'd been lifted across the curve of the davit above me and I could see the part-corpse was wearing bright new American baseball boots, just like the ones Tolliver had bought in Charleston last week.

I remember feeling terribly sad, and maybe a little angry too, at the waste caused by people who started wars. The way beautiful ships were being sunk every day, and radio operators cooked in super-heated instant ovens. And baseball boots were being bought and never getting properly worn out before their owners . . .

'Mister Barton.'

A head inserted itself between me and Tolliver. But I
didn't think it was *his* head, mind . . . Dreamily I giggled,
'They're a load of bull, Spanish ships are. Jus' a load've bull,
Charlie boy . . .'

'. . . C'MON, Sir! Snap *out*'ve it f'r Chris . . .'

I sat up, staring wildly around as the horror hit me again.
The whole length of the starboard side boat deck housing
was spouting flame suddenly, great red tongues of fire
licking from every port and through half a dozen jagged
gashes while even the funnel had a hole in it, or more of a
tear really, with the exhaust smoke puttering and writhing
uncontrollably along the deck instead of being thrown high
above the ship . . . I blinked at the hose still convulsively
spraying water in a lashing fountain over something lying
sinuously over and around the holocaust – the jumper stay.
Gazing up involuntarily I discovered we'd lost our whole
foretopmast, sheared clean away above the crosstrees, which
meant we'd lost our wireless H.T. aerial as well.

But we'd already lost the bloody wireless, come to that.
With the rest of the ship about to follow . . .

'I was getting dressed f'r my watch,' Third Mate Ainslie
said in a wondering tone. 'Then there was a bang, sort of . . .
an' I just stepped clean out of my berth on to the boat deck.
Jus' stepped clean *through* where the bulkhead had been . . .
are you O.K. now?'

'The bridge,' I whispered doggedly. 'We've got to stop
her.'

Just as an irate figure came charging furiously around the
corner. But there was only time to recognize Bosun Fletcher's unaccustomedly athletic bulk propelled on a wave of
raging epithets before the Third Mate choked, 'Oh God,
here it comes again!'

He flung himself down beside me as the express train in
the sky halted abruptly for the second time. I retained one
stark image of Fletcher frozen parallel and three feet above

the deck in an immaculate swallow-dive for cover . . . then shielded my head with my arms, screwing my eyes tight as a shipowner's wallet while the concussions swamped and reverberated all around me.

And under me. Smashing through the *Maya Star*'s hull this time too.

Until finally I dragged myself on to what felt like columns of aspic, heard the gun on our poop give yet another bloody-minded *slam*, snarled, 'I don't believe it. I don't bloody *believe* it . . .' and started running along the same old path to the bridge . . .

Quartermaster Tennison met me at the top of the ladder.

Though perhaps waited for me was a more apt description, because Tennison didn't have any legs left. Yet he didn't look so gloomy any more either. There was still that expression of . . . almost of vindication, in a way. Like he'd worn earlier when the raider first revealed itself, as if the anticipation of your own personal nightmare is far worse than the actual living through it when it comes.

Or the dying. During it.

He said calmly, 'The missus an' me, we used ter go walkin' every Sunday. When I wus home, like . . .'

I whirled with the bile welling in the back of my throat. 'Get the Chief Steward up here f'r Christ's sake . . .' I half screamed towards the dazed figures picking themselves off what had been our boat deck once. 'An' the medical chest. The stretcher . . .'

'FIIIIIRE . . . !'

Slam!

'REload! Up five . . .'

The German vessel apparently doing something rather strange all of a sudden. Not precisely abeam any longer but falling back slightly, steaming steadily on our quarter now with the black barrel of Timmer's stern chaser persistently training further and further aft to remain layed on hcr . . . but then a cloud of smoke and exhaust fumes eddied abruptly on a shift of wind, temporarily obscuring my vision astern and I knuckled my eyes savagely, forcing myself to look down at the mutilated man again.

'He'll get a bit've a surprise, Chief Steward will,' the top half of Tennison whispered in black satisfaction. 'Most complicated doctorin' job 'e's had yet was Engineer Nolan's poisoned finger.'

'Easy, Arthur,' I pleaded agitatedly. 'Take it easy, lad.'

But he just gave a sort of funny, sardonic little smile. It didn't fade away for quite a long time and I knew he was dead. I'd started running for the remains of the wheelhouse itself just as Third Mate Ainslie and the Bosun clambered up the buckled ladder behind me.

'Jesus!' the Third breathed. 'Oh Mother've *Jesus*.'

Because the *Maya Star*'s bridge structure simply didn't exist any more. Or nothing that could be recognized as one for, while the wooden frontage had miraculously escaped extinction, all the rest, all the housing and chartroom, had been flattened to a skeleton, topsy-turvy mound of shattered timber and slashed, still-bleeding bags of sand . . . I began clawing frantically at the mess while all the time waiting for the smash of the next incoming salvo. The sweat dripped unrestrainedly into my eyes and I didn't think I'd have any kind of smile on my face when it came my turn to be a piece of a man.

'They've got to be under here,' I snarled, not really knowing myself whether I meant the Old Man and the junior watchkeepers or the engine room telegraphs. Not that they'd be functioning, any of them, and it wouldn't help me to stop the ship, but I still couldn't bring myself to leave the bridge. Not at that moment. Not even to do the logical thing and try to prevent this continuing slaughter.

So we simply burrowed like men possessed, with bleeding fingers and shoulders hunched in fearful anticipation of what must happen in the next few seconds, when the raider fired again.

'HERE!' Fletcher yelled.

I scrambled over on my hands and knees and helped him ease the heavy slab of concrete on end. For a stupefied intake of breath I wondered who'd trussed Fourth Mate Gulliver like a naked fowl before finally gutting him wide open, then I recognized the Aldis cord and turned away savagely. The Bosun let the slab fall back with a crash and swore in a low, flat monotone.

'Gimme a hand f'r God's sake,' Ainslie muttered apprehensively, lying flat across the wreckage and reaching into it as far as he could. We tore at the protruding end of the wheelhouse door until it slid to one side with a tinkling of glass fragments. I urged, 'Can you get in now?' and the Third Mate said, 'I'll try . . .'

He squeezed his head and one arm into the cavity and groped blindly. Then he stopped, holding himself rigid until gradually his shoulders began to heave spasmodically. 'Get me out,' he half-screamed. 'Get me OUT f'r Chris . . .'

But we'd found the Old Man. And the boy.

As well as the amputated brass column of the engine room telegraph. All together. In a very small space . . . I got slowly to my feet and, just for a moment, closed my eyes and allowed the wind to play on my face while feeling the ship move under me with the same easy motion she'd displayed over tens of thousands of sea miles before.

Fletcher said anxiously, 'Captain,' and it took me a little time to realize he meant me.

And then somebody began shouting from the boat deck, or bellowing really in a furious torrent of abuse, but I didn't move right away even then. Mrs Prethero would have been horrified if I hadn't permitted her husband at least a modicum of respect before taking command of the *Maya Star*.

And of all who sailed in her. Whole men, part men, frightened men and men who still didn't know when they were beaten . . . I walked back to the starboard ladder and looked down blankly. It didn't seem quite decent, somehow, to be making all that fuss with the old captain just dead, and the new one still grieving.

But then I found that grief took many forms. And that I didn't have a monopoly of sadness.

There was a great flowering gash in the side of the Fourth Engineer's head, and his once-white overalls were all red down one leg as he tried to drag himself towards us on a string of imprecations. When he saw me staring over he spat with a terrible contempt.

'Bastards!' he sobbed. 'You bastards up there killed 'em. The whole bloody watch below on the control platform . . . a shell come on through an' . . .'

It seemed so unfair. Which made it just like the rest of the bloody war.

And then the sky finally did tear apart again, a rushing, demented bedlam of displaced air. I was protesting and going down on the deck and hearing the accusing scream from under me all at the same time.

'. . . bits've them . . . no orders after stand-by was rung down . . . still full ahead an' . . .'

A concertina of explosions. The ship rearing away like a shying animal. Flame . . . expanding balls of fire jetting and mushrooming in great licking tongues under a canopy of screeching, tumbling splinters and parts of rails and ventilators and boats . . . I sensed Fourth Engineer Roberts being blown away on a long fading arc of shrieking hatred and hoped he hadn't used it all up on the *Maya Star*'s bridge complement . . that he'd saved at least a little. For the men *behind* the guns over there.

Virtually the whole of the starboard side boat deck was ablaze now as I hauled my eyes above the level of the scarred rail. Both boats had completely vanished this time, along with Roberts and the elegantly shod corpse of Ordinary Seaman Tolliver . . . I shaded my eyes from the crackling heat and tried to find the raider through the shimmering haze which curtained the bridge from that section of sea.

From behind me the Bosun growled, 'Where the hell *are*

they, then?' but I could only shake my head numbly because I couldn't see another ship anywhere out there.

And then there was a familiar *slam* from our poop – which inferred that at least our own personal Bombardier David still had some kind of Teutonic Goliath in view, apart from also having the kind of sod's luck which only shines on the outrageously defiant.

Just before the Third Mate crawled over and said wonderingly, 'She's going away. They're bloody well running *away* for God's sake.'

I couldn't help smiling. All that shambles and death surrounding me and I still couldn't help smiling a bit. 'You sure, Three Oh,' I retorted sardonically. 'You sure she isn't wanting to surrender to us?'

But then I caught sight of her myself, through the flames, and the smile gradually erased itself as my mouth sagged vacantly. Because the yellow-funnelled raider really *was* steaming away from us, just as Ainslie said. Actually presenting her stern and drawing away on a steady heading for the distant haze.

Then, suddenly, I understood.

'She's not running,' I yelled. `*We* are. It's us still turning to port while Jerrie's holding his course.'

We stared at each other blankly while the ship burned and the untended engines continued to drive us in an uncontrollable slow circle, and the grey sea separating us from the enemy warship grew wider and wider and, at the same time, seemingly more angry. Heaving spitefully as if in frustration.

Over a mile and a half now. And still increasing.

'It don't make no sense, dammit,' the Bosun snorted. *Slam!*

The report from Timmer's gun jerked me out of my dazed speculation. 'Maybe it does,' I muttered. 'That hit Timmer scored on her – it must have jammed their steering gear. It could be that their rudder's wedged at midships an' all they can do is . . .'

36

'Look OUT!' Ainslie choked.

And we all hugged the deck once again in the knowledge that the raider *did* have one more thing she could do while we were still within range. And that she was doing it.

Certainly there weren't as many hits on us as before. For one thing the German vessel could only bring her after armament to bear as the angle between us opened, and also we ourselves offered a smaller target now, only our stern profile exposed to her gunners.

But that was enough.

The shock wave literally drove us ahead this time, punching the after end of the centrecastle in a sledge-hammer sparkle of explosions. I felt the ship reel convulsively, sliding part-round in a violent sheer as though we'd been pooped by a heavy following sea. One, maybe two rounds exploded in the water alongside the bridge to lift a great hissing deluge of cordite-tainted sea inboard and on top of us.

Ainslie was the first to drag himself above the level of the rail. I remember crawling in a daze on hands and knees, listening to the odd sound of water racing and gurgling through a hundred splintered gaps before cascading back down to the sea below, and then the Third Mate's shout.

'The gun! They've knocked out the gun!'

I hauled myself upright with a supreme effort of will. The heat from the boat deck fires flayed my face and I shielded my eyes in momentary panic until I managed to focus them through the flickering haze.

And then stiffened as the full impact of the scene astern struck me. Oh, the gun was finished just like Ainslie had said. I could tell that instantly by the way the long barrel now dipped disconsolately towards the sea, immobile and bowed almost as if in defeat. The crew were still around it though, but not fighting any more, all sprawled in untidy, foetal attitudes like sleeping children apart from one solitary figure – Timmer – stumbling towards the ready-use locker with dogged, flash-blinded persistence.

I could still make out the fog-blurred silhouette of a very frustrated *Kriegsmarine* commerce raider too, steadily disappearing into the grey murk on a billowing trail as the fire in her damaged steering compartment apparently prevented her from coming back at us for the final kill.

The double-edged irony of war. Ironic because now her German captain would probably never know, never be absolutely sure of how much damage he'd inflicted on the sitting duck which had so disconcertingly insisted on flying away and, even more outrageously, on pecking back with bloody-minded precision.

And double-edged . . . ? Well, that was why I'd stiffened as I looked astern after that last petulant salvo.

Because that was the moment when I saw the Angel of Death creeping out of number five hold.

Looking for all the world like a little puff of smoke.

I began running.

I'd always seemed to be running, though, for that matter. Ever since the raider had first pounced I'd been running like a madman. Apart from the odd times when I'd been lying down instead, that was, simply clutching my ears against the violence of the attack on the *Maya Star*.

Only now there wasn't any attack in progress, and the raider was virtually out of range and sight – yet I was still bloody well *running*.

And more scared and apprehensive than I'd ever been, even at the height of the action.

So it wasn't entirely surprising that Ainslie and the Bosun were staring at me with the same sort of expressions I'd seen once before, on the faces of Jeremy Prethero and poor bloody Tennison that time when I'd flown into the wheel-house to slam the telegraph to 'Stand by'.

Dead shattered, and uneasy with it.

I snapped tightly, 'Number *five* hold,' skidding to cross the shambles that had been a wheelhouse once but now formed a crypt for condensed men.

Fletcher called placatingly, 'Easy, Mister Barton . . . what about number five then?'

'It's on FIRE!'

'*Christ!*'

I could have sworn they overtook me on the straight leading to the head of the port ladder, yet by the time we'd actually reached the bottom we were neck and neck again – and while it may only have been my imagination there really did seem to be what looked suspiciously like a footprint on the back of the Bosun's tattered shirt.

But just for the duration of that crazed, black-comedy moment of panic my mind had ground to a dead stop, unable to cope any longer with the pressures building relentlessly within. There were so many problems, so many actions requiring simultaneous attention . . . the ship still steaming on a blind, juggernauting course to nowhere; most, if not all of our engine room staff dead and unable to halt our eighteen knot rampage . . . and that in its turn meant we couldn't lower a single lifeboat – even if there were enough crewmen left alive to man the falls in the first place, dammit!

Our telemotor steering gear was gone, leaving only a remote after emergency position which demanded time – and more hands – to bring into operation. Casualties . . . men wounded, shocked, burned . . . perhaps trapped even now in the fires rampaging through the cabins. Soon it would spread from the starboard side to this port area – and then we'd have no boats at all anyway . . .

. . . and now the ultimate threat. My whispering, curling Angel of Death. Because the *Maya Star* wasn't simply burning above decks any more, now apparently she had a deeper, more immediately lethal conflagration in her belly. In number five hold.

While next to number five lay number six.

Containing 200 tons of 6-inch calibre naval gun ammunition, 180 tons of 4-inch, 125 tons of assorted small calibre plus several cased aerial bombs and an uncomfortably large volume of a substance consisting of nitro-glycerine and gun cotton dissolved in acetone and stabilized with a small proportion of Vaseline. The Royal Navy called it cordite. I just called it bloody dangerous.

Especially when someone lit a fire. Right beside it . . .

3

Oh, not that the cargo in the *Maya Star*'s aftermost hold was all *that* exclusive, mind you.

I mean we had virtually a carbon-copy selection of fragmentation bombs, grenades, torpedoes, land mines and other assorted killing devices stowed in numbers one and three cargo spaces as well. In fact while we weren't strictly classed as an ammunition ship we were still a bloody good imitation of one.

Which was why my nerves were more than a little frayed by the time I arrived on the relatively undamaged port side boat deck and why, when I finally realized that newly materialized and familiar faces were watching my undignified panic, I didn't let them see my relief at discovering we still had at least a part crew left so much as vent the frustrated anger that just had to get out somehow.

By grinding to an abrupt halt, staring savagely at the anxious group of survivors, and snarling, 'An' where the hell have *you* lot been, then. Or were you here by the boats as soon's you heard the first shot fired, eh?'

For a moment nobody moved, then a figure stepped forward with difficulty. He was all burned down one side and I didn't even recognize him at first until he answered bitterly, 'On my way down below, where I should've been . . .'

He gestured painfully at A. B. Toomey and another two seamen standing behind him. 'They came down an' got me out, you stupid brassbound bastard,' the Second Engineer continued. 'An' it took real guts. Especially for a deckie.'

'We were wi' the Bose's deck-wash party, me an' Ricketts here,' Able Seaman Cleese muttered defensively. 'The first round took Ernie Tolliver's 'ead clean off've 'is shoulders an' sparked me out. Ricketts dragged me under cover till I come round . . .'

'I'm sorry,' I said, guilty as hell at my own inadequacy. I'd had no right to turn on them, I was as frightened and as apprehensive as any man aboard the *Maya Star* at that moment.

'An' I wus in the galley,' the last man – a black man – growled unmollified. And then I realized it wasn't a black man in front of me but Second Cook Gifford. '. . . fryin' up the soddin' breakfasts, Mister. Until them bastid Jerries put one through the coke stove an' the Chief Chef . . .'

'I'm *sorry*,' I said again, a little more petulantly this time. But it wasn't a very good start to being a captain. Then a flurry of smoke blew over from the starboard side and we began to choke convulsively. 'It's gettin' dodgy, i'nt it?' someone muttered uneasily. 'Bloody dodgy.'

I rubbed my eyes and peered into the group. 'Anyone seen the Second Mate yet?'

'He's in there, along wi' the rest've the watch below,' a seaman grunted, jerking his thumb at the steel plating of the accommodation. I could see the paint blistering as the confined heat built to furnace temperature and felt sick.

'The Chief Steward went in to help,' another voice offered quietly. 'He never come out again either.'

I bit my lip. There had been fifty-four men in our crew, yet I could only see seven in front of me. Plus Ainslie and the Bosun . . . maybe Chippie and young Meehan still on the foredeck and whatever members of the gun's crew remaining alive on the poop . . . say ten to fifteen survivors – unless any others turned up by some miracle. I looked over their heads and saw the Angel of Death again, only it was bigger now, even more threatening.

'Number five's on fire,' I said, keeping my tone as level as I could.

'Oh *shit!*' Second Cook Gifford muttered. Blackly.

Able Seaman Ricketts looked blank. But Able Seaman Ricketts always looked blank. 'What's so speshul about

42

number five, then?'

'Nothin',' Bosun Fletcher shrugged. 'It's what's next to it that's special, lad.'

'Stick yer fingers in yer ears an' you'll never find out,' suggested Cleese sourly. There was a faint ripple of laughter from the group. But only very faint.

'All right, that's enough . . .' I whirled on Second Engineer Nolan, trying not to see how badly burned he was. 'Will there still be hose pressure in the deck lines, Archie?'

He winced as the ship rolled sullenly and his arm brushed against the man next to him. 'Should be. Unless they've been blown away somewhere and venting the system.'

'We'll have to check . . . Bosun.'

'Aye?'

'Take four lads and rig hoses on the well deck. See what you can do about the source in five but put a sprayer into number six first, keep the cargo cool. Maybe the blast's taken the hatch boards off anyway but, if it hasn't, be careful for God's sake . . . You O.K. now, Gifford?'

The Second Chef shrugged. 'I'd be better if I wasn't 'ere.'

I managed a weak grin. 'Join the club. Go with the Bosun. See what you can do for the blokes at the gun . . . Mister Ainslie.'

The Third Mate stepped forward with alacrity. 'Keep Ricketts and Toomey here. Lower these two boats to prom deck level and see they're properly stored and equipped. Then search the ship for casualties . . .'

A dull explosion shook the accommodation. A glass scuttle blew outwards in a spray of glass fragments while a jet of flame licked and curled upwards through the aperture. Abruptly Second Wireless Operator Martin backed out of the door leading to the radio room alleyway looking sick as a dog and I bit my lip savagely, feeling the same way – I'd completely forgotten he'd been in there trying to fight the fire all on his own.

Seeing the youngster was at the end of his tether I began

to move towards him until Bosun Fletcher, leading his party at a gallop past the shocked wireless man, called calmly, 'Mornin', Second Operator.'

Martin jerked his head up, returned an automatic 'G'morning, Bose,' then frowned and looked a bit mystified. He wasn't quite as pale, though. There's nothing like casual normality to bring you back to . . . well . . . to normal.

Ainslie gestured towards the already swung-out boats. 'Leggo the gripes, Ricketts. Toomey, you check out the water containers . . .'

I gazed anxiously outboard. We were still turning in a wide circle to port while the visibility was steadily clamping down to around two miles now, but I wasn't too worried about the risk of collision. We were very unlikely to meet anyone else this far offshore – apart from that bloody raider, of course. And I didn't think she'd be able to find us very easily again in this murk, not even if she got her steering repaired and reckoned it was worth while.

Anyway now there was that even more immediate threat – the fire in five. Because if we couldn't extinguish *that* in the next few minutes . . . I turned and looked anxiously at the Second Engineer, now leaning weakly against the ladder with his good side. He was trembling convulsively and I guessed shock was taking hold, but he seemed to be the only engineer we had left apart from one greaser, a not-particularly bright rating called Hotchkiss. And even Hotchkiss had been a member of the gun's crew the last time I saw him.

'How're you feeling, Archie?'

'Guilty. I gather you're the captain now, an' I just called you a brassbound bastard.'

'An' you were entitled to . . .' I gestured at the steadily growing column of smoke from aft. 'I don't think we've got much time. Can you manage to get back below and stop her?'

The brave smile faded a little. 'I was afraid you were going to ask me that.'

44

'*Can* you? We may have to abandon pretty soon and it's not possible. Not at eighteen knots.'

But the Second was already limping away, back towards the engine room entrance and what would be, for him, agony-laden flights of near-vertical steel ladders. And what remained of his colleagues spread around the sweltering bowels of the ship.

'Amend that apology,' he grunted. 'Now I only take back the brassbound bit!'

Sparks came over and said quietly, 'I'll go with him, Sir.'

I could have pointed out that he wouldn't have a hope in hell, neither him nor Archie Nolan, if she blew while they were down there. Until I remembered that the ammunition was stowed throughout the whole length of the ship anyway, and reflected bleakly that it wouldn't make much difference where any of us were when it did happen.

'There aren't any *girls* down there, you know,' I said with mock severity.

The youngster didn't quite manage a grin, but he didn't look quite so upset either. 'You can't really blame them for leaving, can you?' he retorted solemnly.

I'd just opened my mouth to add something reassuring . . . then I happened to glance aft, over his shoulder, blurted a ridiculously formal 'Excuse me . . .' instead. And began running.

Again.

But I'd just noticed the underside of my climbing, smoky Angel once more. Only now it had a flickering, reddish tinge to it and any fire burning as brightly as that had to have a lot of heat in it.

I could have sworn the Angel stooped down and touched me as I ran. Cynically welcoming in its acrid embrace.

I picked up two more survivors during my headlong rush towards the after well deck. Or collided with them was probably a more accurate description as I half slid, half fell down the ladder to the main centrecastle deck.

Chippie and junior apprentice Meehan, both steaming full ahead in the same direction as me. The old man looked mad enough to eat nails while the boy positively radiated suppressed excitement. But he hadn't seen the *Maya Star*'s upper decks yet. And what war did to dead men's corpses.

Without slackening speed the Carpenter fell into line astern, waving his gnarled fist in fury and bawling, 'Gimme two minnits wi' yon bristle-'eaded Hun skipper . . . Two *minnits* is all I asks, Lord? Jus' 'im, me, an' me fuckin' *mallet* . . .'

Until we arrived at the break of the centrecastle overlooking the after decks, and I lost track of Chippie's flow of outraged invective, trying desperately to see everything all at once and assess how much time we had left – both for fire-fighting and wishful thinking.

Actually it was the smoke which first took me aback. It didn't look like any kind of angel now, not this close to. More a sort of animated, clinging fuzz which swirled tenaciously in every sheltered pocket, even climbing the after face of the mast until, half way up, the wind finally whirled it astern in frisking, cavorting streamers.

And underneath the smoke, the gaping cavity of number five with twisted metal hatch beams stripped of their covering like some gigantic griddle bridging the blaze, a sullen red glare with a myriad of baby flamelets licking to the grey, refracted sky.

While surrounding the inferno was the blast-torn deck itself – a battleground of fragmented hatch boards and cargo spewed by the force of the hit. Spilled cases of bully beef mingling with the polished steel glint of Seattle-manufactured machine tools; crushed coils of barbed wire intertwined with spools of telephone cable; tank tracks all dusted with a thick yellow layer of dried egg powder sucked from the breached tween deck. Chicago hides, chili beans, flowering bales of kapok . . . a mad storekeeper's nightmare . . .

Unthinkingly I slid down the ladder rails on my hands,

46

my feet raised fractionally above the treads. It was only after I'd collapsed at the bottom that I realized most of the bloody ironwork had been shot away, but I scrambled up and picked my way urgently through the mess towards the Bosun and his gang.

Fletcher roared, 'Water ON then . . . ! Christ but she's cookin' already, Mister Barton. Watch yerself!'

The white threadline of hose beside me abruptly pulsated as the pressure slammed through. There was a broken splutter at the nozzle then the two seamen gripping it braced against the backlash of the jet. Steam billowed out of the hold, swirling and joining with the smoke.

Chippie arrived, still muttering, and the three of us leaned cautiously over the coaming, staring down into the hold. I put my mouth against Fletcher's ear and yelled above the din, 'We got tyres stowed after tween deck. Smells like they're burning . . .'

The Bosun nodded and ducked at the same time as a blast of heat roared out and upward. I wasn't so quick, my eyebrows felt as if they'd shrivelled before I finally fell back. Chippie began to move towards the still battened-down number six. 'You wants ter get a sprayer in there, Bosun. Thought you'd've known that much wi'out *me* havin' to tell yer.'

Fletcher turned purple. 'I DO know, ye dodderin' old bugger! Jus' open the hatch an' let me do the thinkin' . . .'

I rubbed my eyes wearily and prayed, 'Dear God, don't let them start again. Not now. Not with all the rest've my worries . . .' because Bosun Fletcher and the Carpenter had argued consistently across every ocean in the whole bloody world. Back and forward, from Hong Kong to Spitzbergen, the Panama to the Suez – endlessly and heatedly disputing every fact from who was the hardest drinking sailorman to who'd got the prior right to the bottom berth in their shared cabin.

Even last night had seen them bickering – this time about who'd lived through the hottest weather a sailorman could

47

ever be called on to endure.

'I wus A.B. in the ol' *Tantalus* once,' the Bosun had challenged preparing his blockbuster with the relish of an already foregone victor. 'Nineteen thirty two, in the Indian Ocean. An' it wus so *hot* the cook never 'ad to light the galley stove f'r five days . . . jus' put the vittles raw on the plates an' they fried up beautiful, layin' on the deck jus' outside've the galley door.'

But Chippie had simply snorted, eyeing his adversary with devastating scorn. 'I seen blokes wearin' scarves an' *gloves* in weather cool as that, Bosun . . . Now when I wus shipped out on the windjammer *Katy Hay* in '28 the chef couldn't even *'old* the plates, they wus so 'ot. Excep' once, now I think of it. 'E did try an' cook once, I remember . . .'

'Oh aye,' growled the Bosun despite himself. 'What 'appened then, Carpenter?'

But Fletcher always had been a sucker for leading with his chin. And Chippie was merciless. Without even a shred of embarrassment or shame.

'Chef tried makin' custard,' he'd averred, face straight as a probationary cherub's. 'Until the wooden ladle 'e wus stirrin' with . . . it burst inter flames in 'is 'and.'

. . . which brought me back to the Motor Vessel *Maya Star*. And the year 1941. On probably the hottest day *I'd* ever be likely to see in my life.

And *that* didn't strike me as being a very long term proposition, either. Not right at that moment . . .

A second hose line splurged into life, sweeping the flames away with battering over-kill. Only, as soon as the jet sheered to either side, playing a predatory game of hide and seek with the rest of the blaze, all the little flames sprang back up again, hissing great clouds of steam and flying ash flakes in positive glee.

And then I noticed the water lying on the deck where I stood. Pools of it supporting a scum of soot and charred embers and little yellow ochre islands of slowly reconstituting egg powder . . . and if you looked hard enough you could just make out the haze rising from each pool as the water heated up, gradually coming to the boil.

Which meant the fire was already below us, the seat of the conflagration widening, eating steadily into the cargo-packed sides of the upper tween decks . . .

I turned to young Apprentice Meehan and kept my voice casual. 'Nip up and give Mister Ainslie a hand on the boat deck, will you? Give him my compliments, ask him if he could hurry as much as possible in lowering the boats to embarkation level.'

The boy squeaked, 'Aye, *aye*, Sir,' in a terribly important manner and scurried forward with a real square rig set to his thin shoulders. I called, ' . . . and get yourself a lifejacket from the prom deck locker, laddie,' then turned to face the poop and the dismally angled gun. Any stretcher casualties had to be prepared and put aboard the boats now.

I could see Second Cook Gifford kneeling beside a still figure crumpled at the edge of the platform. Two more men sat with bowed heads, leaning against the ready-use ammunition locker, and I recognized one as Timmer – Bombardier Timmer, by God! Still apparently unmarked and under the protection of that great sod's law which smiled down on the brave. And the stupid.

Sometimes . . .

Because there was also blood trickling freely over one side of the steel deck, certainly far too much to have come from one man, soldier or sailor. Or not from a living one, anyway. I threw a hasty glance towards the men now struggling to roll back the tarpaulin from the square of number six, then ran towards the ladder to the poop. Minutes were vital for our cargo – but seconds could also help the survival of a badly wounded man.

Gifford looked up sharply as I breasted the top, then calmly returned to his self-imposed task of binding a tourniquet around the hideously torn stump of what had been Steward Thomson's left arm. His attitude didn't surprise me, the Second Cook had always been a truculent, invariably resentful member of the *Maya Star*'s crew who'd only just managed to toe the thin line between bare respect and outright insubordination ever since he'd first joined the ship in Liverpool. But he'd also been strangely helpful to the Chief Steward when any first aid had been called for. Odd really, for a man like I had him placed as.

'Two dead an' one missin' – probably blown ower the wall,' he volunteered stolidly. 'The Corporal an' Greaser Hotchkiss is shocked, Clayton's got 'alf his guts shot away, Willie Sproat an' the Lamptrimmer wi' nasty 'ead wounds an' that's the lot . . . 'cept Thomson here. Lucky it weren't yer right mitt, Reggie boy. Couldn't drop the wife a line to let 'er know you're comin' home if it'd been yer right arm, could yer?'

The suddenly one-armed man didn't even flicker an eyelid, though. He just slumped there with his face a mask of shock and pain, while there was that same sense of . . . of astonishment in it. Just like the Chief Radio Operator had worn while the shell cremated him.

'Thomson is . . . was left-handed,' I muttered bitterly. 'Can I do anything for Clayton, Chef?'

He tied the binding off, then began to tear his own striped apron into strips. Unless the engine room emergency kit could be found they would be the nearest thing to bandages we had available.

'You got other problems. I'll look after 'im in a minute.'

'But can you *do* anything? On your own?'

Gifford's soot-shiny face turned towards me momentarily. 'Yeah. I c'n hold his hand, Mister Barton . . . Until 'e dies.'

A shaky voice called 'Sir,' from behind and I swung to find Timmer pulling himself to his feet. The soldier swayed fractionally and I lunged to help him but he shook his head, breathing deeply.

'I shouldn't've done it, should I, Sir? Fired without orders.'

I opened my mouth to answer. I think I'd meant to say a lot of things to him, hard things, about order and discipline

50

and authority, an' just who the hell did he think was running this bloody ship because whoever it was it certainly *wasn't* a two-stripe bloody pongo . . . ! Then I saw the look in his eyes as he gazed around the poop, and over the bits and pieces the raider's salvo had left of his gun crew, until finally they halted on the two mutilated corpses impacted against the starboard rail. Both had been wearing khaki denim issue. Once.

So I simply shook my head – not too reprovingly though – then added, 'They would have opened fire anyway, Timmer. They heard us transmitting against their orders.'

He blinked suddenly, tearing his eyes away from the bodies with an effort and focusing them on me. I noticed he was still wearing his glasses and felt a flicker of surprise that they'd stayed intact through the explosion – then I remembered the Chief Operator's epaulettes still balancing on naked, flash-charred shoulders and reflected once again on the random selectivity of blast.

'You fought them off actually,' I told him. 'You hit his steering gear and he kept right on going out of the picture. For the present, anyway.'

'You mean they might come back, Sir?'

Startled, I saw the suddenly animated look in his otherwise rather placid face, and the way his eyes turned towards the gun. I had another unsettling memory of the solitary stumbling figure up here a few minutes ago, still trying to fight a whole warship with a smashed weapon and a knocked-out gun crew around him, then shook my head again. Very emphatically indeed.

'No,' I retorted. 'But if I'm wrong, and they do find us again, promise me one thing, Bombardier.'

'Sir?'

'Remember Lord Nelson,' I pleaded wearily. 'Only in your case – turn your blind eye towards the bloody *enemy*.'

I hurried back down to the well deck. Behind me Timmer began to shake Greaser Hotchkiss into startled awareness while Second Cook Gifford had moved over to the horrifically wounded Clayton. Now he was kneeling there, a hard-bitten rough-tongued dockside tearaway who'd given very little to the ship since he'd first joined.

Yet now he was using one calloused hand to cradle a dying seaman's head. While the other, ever so gently, prevented the boy's intestines from slipping out through a gaping shrapnel slash.

I rejoined the Bosun and the Carpenter just as they slid one corner section of the heavy hatch boards back with a crash.

'Lash one o' them hoses in position, Cleese,' Fletcher was panting. 'Break out another an' fix a spray nozzle . . . *Jaldi*, lad!'

The smoke from the adjacent five seemed thicker now, much more oily and I guessed the blaze was consolidating in the section containing those damned heavy duty military tyres. I began to feel even more despondent as I inserted myself between the men staring critically, a little more than apprehensively, into the ammunition-packed depths of number six hold.

It was dark down there, still shielded from the colourless light of that bleak morning by the main hatch covering. But there was more than enough illumination to reveal the cargo lying passively waiting for a violent and explosive end – either singly, through the long gun barrels of the Royal Navy's Simonstown Squadron – or together, all in one stupendous chain-reacting flash as the heat building in the *Maya Star*'s next hold touched off the first solitary round. And then another. And another . . .

'Hurry up wi' that SPRAYER!' roared Bosun Fletcher.

They simply lay there. Row upon row of softly gleaming casings, each separated from its identical twin by a rough cut wooden spar and each nose cone facing forward, the first line almost brushing the steel bulkhead which formed the only barrier between them and the fire.

'They're all six-inch shells stowed that end of the hold,' I muttered, desperately trying to cast my mind back to that uneasy night in Charleston three weeks ago, when I was working on the cargo stowage plan for the next leg of Voyage 16, M.V. *Maya Star*. 'Smaller stuff mostly in the centre section . . . an' those bloody cordite charges in the after part.'

'What about the lower hold, Mister B?'

'General. Nothing explosive. Same with the lower tween deck.'

'MIND YER BACKS . . . !'

Cleese and Deckie Sullivan struggling to haul a new length of hose across the ochre skating rink of the deck. We all grabbed and the bright brass nozzle flopped over the coaming like a dead snake. Sullivan ran back towards the red-painted valve, skidded full length in the mess, scrabbled the rest of the way and spun the wheel on a string of oaths.

Fletcher braced as the pressure came through then jerked his head furiously towards the Carpenter. 'Go *on* then! Open the rest've the hatch you dodderin' ol' bugger . . .'

While Chippie, who was already belting at the wedges like they were the Bosun's head, screamed, 'Don't *you* tell me what ter do, Bosun. Don' you bloody tell ME what ter do!'

Whereupon Third Mate Ainslie arrived on the run from the boat deck, and *he* was snarling, 'Bastards! Scavenging irresponsible *bastards* . . .'

'Mad,' I thought dazedly. 'The whole bloody world's going mad,' as Ainslie continued, 'Compasses . . . charts . . . blanket boxes, barley sugar . . . they've been cleaned out've both boats. Some lousy Yankee longshoreman's lifted every damn thing!'

I gazed at him as the full impact of the revelation slowly sank in. For now it not only meant we were aboard a runaway time bomb and two hundred miles from the nearest land, but also we'd apparently lost every piece of navigation equipment we'd carried in our boats – and the *Maya Star*'s primary aids were already wrecked and useless, buried along with her captain in that morgue of a bridge.

'Who checked 'em after we sailed?'

'Second Mate,' Ainslie retorted. 'Supposed to have gone over everything after we left. But Donny always was a lazy bone-idle . . .'

But then he broke off abruptly, staring up at the centre-castle. Including the blazing accommodation where Second Officer Bell had been sleeping. And still was.

I saw him swallow involuntarily, and noticed the way his shoulders sagged, so I said quickly, 'Forget it. We'll manage. Everything else ready to go?'

He shrugged. 'Whenever you are, Sir. Ricketts and Toomey are tackling the fire while they're waiting. Young Meehan's scouting around for lifejackets though most've 'em are either burned or shot up.'

'Like the crew,' I reflected savagely. 'Just like the bloody crew . . .'

A cloud of acrid smoke swirled downwards, stinging my eyes even more. I turned away sharply and found myself looking at the desolate area of the poop once again. Gifford was still kneeling beside the fatally wounded Clayton but the bespectacled Bombardier had managed to rouse Hotchkiss and now they were bending to treat the last two survivors of the gun gang, the two head wounds.

'We'll have to start moving the wounded to embarkation level soon as poss . . .'

Then I broke off suddenly. Something was different – felt different. The same as it had done that time in the radio room . . . and then I smiled hopefully for the first time since we'd sighted a strange ship with a yellow funnel, a whole lifetime ago.

'We're slowing,' I blurted in relief. 'The Second's managed to stop engines . . .'

'Captain!'

I just kept the grin on my face for a moment, not realizing the shout applied to me. Then I heard it again – 'Mister *Barton*!' – and swung to see Fletcher gesturing anxiously. There wasn't any kind of smile on *his* sweat-smeared features though. Not even a flicker of one.

Ainslie and I hurried across while the old familiar fear began to prickle the hairs at the nape of my neck. We looked over the coaming. The shells were still sitting placidly, a little threateningly certainly but now at least there was a fine spray of seawater playing constantly over the ranks. I frowned doubtfully. There didn't seem to be anything happening which hadn't happened already.

'I don't think we got much time,' the old Bosun said very, very quietly indeed. And then he directed the spray away, further into the hold.

It didn't take more than a few moments to see what he meant.

Because the damp residue left on the first row of six-inch ammunition began to steam very soon after.

Evaporating. Like water from a heating-up griddle.

4

I remember standing there by the open square of number six and looking forward, up at the ship herself, and seeing only a nightmare of devastation in the gutted and blazing starboard upper-deck, and the shapeless tangle that had been our bridge, and the crooked, torn funnel overshadowing a blasted jumble of davits and rails and unidentifiable things.

Hopelessly my eyes travelled downwards, down the after end of the centrecastle under its wartime garb of grey, with the shell bursts from the raider forming a ghastly, riddled pox across every level. Then down even further to where we stood with the flames now leaping high out of number five hold and the smoke and the steam and the roar of the fire below, and all the erupted, smashed stuff of our existence lying around in a monstrous, contaminated omelette of destruction . . .

I lashed out furiously with my foot, sending a crushed scatter of tinned bully beef helter-skelter across the mire. 'Bloody *war* . . . !' I roared incoherently. 'Bloody soddin' rotten WAR . . .'

But it didn't make any difference at all. The flames still flickered and danced against the slow roll of the ship, and the black smoke still rolled skywards carrying the souls of two score murdered sailormen.

While the last whisps of steam hung over the lyddite-charged casings which could mean more appalling deaths at any moment, leaving no memories at all of the *Maya Star*'s last voyage.

Maybe even in the next few seconds . . .

'We're abandoning the ship.' I snapped bitterly. 'Just leave everything and comb through what's left for survivors

. . . Mister Ainslie – have the wounded gun crew put aboard the boats, then lower them as soon as way comes off the ship. Bosun.'

'Aye, Sir?'

'See that Sparks and the Second are out of the engine room. Make sure there's no one left alive down there, then check for . . .'

Bombardier Timmer swung down the ladder from the poop and hurried over, looking down at the ammunition.

'Oh dear,' he said. Even despite the strain I could see Chippie wincing at the somewhat limited descriptive powers of academic pongoes.

'You're a gunner?' I asked anxiously. 'How long d'you reckon before they go up, Timmer?'

He placed his forefinger on the bridge of his spectacles and wrinkled his nose like a speculative rabbit. 'I don't really know, Sir. I've never tried to light one before.'

'Thank you *very* much, Bombardier,' I growled heavily and turned back to Fletcher. '. . . then check forr'ad to see nobody's be . . .'

I stopped.

Bombardier Timmer had hoisted himself over the coaming and had lowered himself down on to the first layer of shells. 'If I pass this up can one of you chaps take the strain, please?'

I pivoted. Very slowly. Timmer was standing legs astride, arms bent at the elbows and gradually going more and more red in the face under the weight of the first round. There was a shuffling of feet behind me as the rest of the group, with one accord, moved back. Strangely, even under those circumstances it suddenly struck me that it was the first time I'd ever seen Chippie and the Bosun agree about anything. Wholeheartedly.

I said, in a slightly wavering but immensely reasonable voice, 'Timmer. Put it down gently. There's a good lad.'

He frowned. 'But hadn't we better get started, Sir? The hotter they get, the more unstable they become and . . . well

'. . . they might explode, you know.'

'Oh,' I muttered, looking as though I'd never actually thought of *that*. Then it was my turn to frown. 'Get started on what?'

'Unloading them out of this place. It's getting a bit too warm, Sir.'

'Timmer . . . there are two hundred *tons* of them underneath you. And that's only the big stuff . . .'

He was beginning to sag and I could see the shell slowly dipping. Nose downwards. 'Please take this, Sir . . . And I only suggest we dump the first two rows – the ones hard against the wall . . .'

'Bulkhead,' I corrected absently.

'Sir?'

'Bulkhead. Your wall's a bulkhead, Bombardier.'

'Yessir. And that would give us a clear space of about five feet to protect the rest of the room . . .

I didn't say his 'room' was a hold. It didn't seem terribly important right at that moment. And his shell had finally come to rest on the pointed end which, even though I knew was unfused, still didn't strike me as being the most sensible way to treat an explosive device, hot or cold.

There didn't seem to be much else I could do, either, so I leaned over and took the bloody thing from him, grunting as the one hundred pound strain came on my arms.

'Now what?'

'Drop it over the side, Sir.'

I handed it to the Bosun who eyed it as if hypnotized. 'Drop it over the side, Bosun,' I suggested. 'Then get the boats ready before Timmer takes us all up with him.'

'Try not to bang it,' the Bombardier's voice called, almost as an afterthought. 'It'll probably explode if you bang it.'

Fletcher dropped it over the side. Like an egg. Not even Chippie found any fault with the way he did *that* either . . . 'Now get out of there, Bombardier,' I ordered grimly. 'Mister Ainslie – prepare to abandon ship as soon as possible please.'

But the Third Mate hesitated. 'I suppose we *couldn't* clear a break between the fire and the ammo . . . Then hang a hatch tarp down the exposed face. Keep it wetted down with a sprayer . . . ?'

I glanced up at the movement on the poop. Second Cook Gifford was slowly descending the ladder. There was a lot of blood on him but the impassive features were as hard as ever. 'Clayton's dead,' he growled flatly. 'An' the two head wounds is pretty bad. *I* can't treat 'em . . . I don't even 'ave a box o' bloody Elastoplast.'

'What about Thomson's arm?'

'Bone's stickin' out through the stump. An' tendons an' stuff. I dunno – it needs trimmin' off . . . sewin' up. Christ knows what else.'

I closed my eyes wearily and made a quick mental calculation. We were two hundred miles off the Brazilian coast. Under the prevailing weather conditions we'd be lucky to average two knots in the lifeboats, and that without any currents setting against us. Which, in turn, meant a minimum of eight days to land – and probably twice that time in actual practice. Even under a tropical sun there should be a good chance for most of us to make it, though maybe only after intense suffering – but not the already injured.

I opened my mouth to order 'Abandon ship', then shut it again. I didn't have the courage to do that any more, not when it meant I was acting as God, because doing so would condemn at least three of my crew, and most probably the badly burned Second Engineer as well, to a horrible lingering death.

'What d'you reckon, Three Oh?' I muttered quietly to Ainslie.

He ran his fingers through his hair and looked tired. 'There's a chance the fire in five'll burn itself out eventually,' he brooded. 'I don't think it's likely to burn lower down into the rest of the hold if we can keep a sort of water table under it at tween deck level.'

'And we've got steel plates stowed after end of four,' I speculated. 'That should prevent it from spreading to that space.'

The ship was only coasting now, gently slipping through the water with a hardly noticeable roll. I turned to face the expectantly watching faces. I'd made my decision.

'I'm staying,' I said as calmly as I could. 'And the wounded will stay too, along with one lifeboat. It's their only chance . . . and if we do go up they won't suffer. They won't even know. But the rest of you have a choice . . . You can take the other boat away and lie off until either the ammo's dumped and the fire cools down, or the ship blows an' you've got a two hundred mile sail ahead of you. The other alternative is you stay aboard – and break your backs humping one hundred pound bombs that'll probably go off in your arms.'

There was a silence for a moment, and quite a lot of uncomfortable shuffling, with everybody looking surreptitiously sideways at everybody else.

'Any man who abandons goes with my blessing,' I added flatly. 'Any man who stays aboard is an absolute bloody fool!'

Bombardier Timmer cleared his throat diffidently. 'I would prefer to remain, Sir. Those little boats look rather dangerous to me.' I nodded. 'Thank you. I'll be glad of your advice . . . Mister Ainslie?' The Third Mate shrugged. 'I just get seasick in a lifeboat anyway.'

Bosun Fletcher stepped forward aggressively and my heart sank. 'You tellin' us it's only bloody fools would stay, Mister Barton?'

'In my candid opinion, yes!'

He began to grin triumphantly. 'Then that means the Carpenter 'asn't got no choice, don't it? I'll have ter stay an' look after the silly old bastid.'

Chippie's brows met in an outraged glower. 'Me leave? You wouldn't get me *in* one o' them boats alongside you, Bosun. I only goes in lifeboats when they's got *proper* bloody seamen innem!'

I had to smile back. And I couldn't help blinking, too. Just a little. 'Gifford?'

The Second Cook looked as truculent as ever. 'I didn't sign articles to ship aboard a rowin' boat. An' someone's gotter do somethin' about the steward's arm – trim it up a bit an' that . . . but I'm goin' ter complain to the Union! I'm tellin' you straight, Mister Barton, soon as I get shore-side I'm seein' the Union about this.'

'Let's get at it then,' Seaman Cleese urged nervously. 'But God 'elp me if the ship goes up an' the wife gets to hear about it. She'll give me hell . . .'

So we began to try to save the *Maya Star*. Not one man among us went away in the boats.

Not even Apprentice Meehan. When I tried to make him stand off in the motor boat, just for a little while until the ship was safe, his lower lip finally trembled so much I had to relent.

It had promised to be the most tearful mutiny a captain ever had to face.

As I said, each shell weighed around a hundred pounds.

They were smothered in grease, designed to slip out of your arms like an oiled piglet, were ringed with brightly painted codings which seemed to smear off against your chest as you clutched them and steadily increased in weight until, by the time you'd lifted twenty or so, they felt like a two ton load. They got warmer, too. Each one that passed through your hands seemed just a little bit hotter than the last . . .

As we cleared the square of the hatch and began to work our way forward, under the turn of the deck, the problems increased. Very soon we were finding difficulty in passing the chain of lyddite-packed obscenities from the cargo level and up over the steel coaming. It only needed one slip, one man's feet to skid from under him, and we would all die. Very suddenly, without even time for a scream, I'd seen an ammunition ship touch off once – she'd been torpedoed just as she'd swung on to the next leg of our North Atlantic convoy zig-zag.

Nothing had happened at first. Just a high, still climbing column of white water forward of her bridge which reached its zenith as the ship steadied on her new heading, then began to fall away in a fine rainbow of hissing spray blowing across her decks.

'Get your battle bowler on,' Jeremy Prethero had said sharply, and I hadn't quite understood what he meant but I'd just slipped the steel helmet over my head anyway, and was nervously adjusting the webbing chin strap when it happened.

She'd slowed down by then, her bows falling away while the next astern – a big grey freighter with decks packed with army trucks and jeeps and light tanks – pulled sharply out of line and started to overtake the stricken victim.

Until suddenly there was a monstrous white light, seemingly in the sea itself, and the whole area around the ammunition carrier appeared to contract, to condense and freeze with the millisecond flash of some submarine magnesium flare, and then during a macabre moment of complete and utter silence through which lines and lines of merchantmen continued steaming as though nothing had ever occurred . . . then the whole midships section of the torpedoed ship opened like a flower while a swirling red ball of fire sort of popped out and rolled up into the sky until suddenly, shockingly, there was only smoke – an expanding island of smoke on the sea with a great black mushroom towering two miles above it.

And only then had come the sound. A sharp report followed by a rumble which rattled the *Maya Star*'s wheelhouse windows uneasily in their frames. Then the debris came as well, plummeting vertically to spatter the decks of the closest ships and smash the skulls of the unwary audience.

A single steel rivet struck the bridge deck between the

captain and myself. Humbly I had bent and picked it up but I didn't hold it for very long. It was still white-hot, even then . . .

Eventually we had to rig the derricks for working the hatch. It seemed to take a lifetime of struggling with black-greased steel wire and bleeding fingers plucking at recalcitrant snatch blocks while, all the time, we saw the hollow white faces of our shipmates around us, each with its own individual expectation of death.

The winches were still operational. Second Engineer Nolan had clambered back down those ladders for a second time, suffering what must have been the agonies of the Inquisition to engage the necessary switches on the main board. Somehow we'd raised a ragged cheer as the first net swung up out of the hold, whisked outboard on a frenetic rattling of churning winch barrels and hung over the sea, swinging gently with the slow roll of the ship.

Almost ceremonially I yanked at the fisherman's style cod-end we'd devised to release the load. The first mini-segment of a potential maxi-detonation fell end over end and disappeared below the surface.

'Only one at a time in the sling remember,' Bombardier Timmer warned deferentially. 'They could be getting a bit unstable now, being hot. It only needs two of 'em to strike a spark and . . .'

We stopped cheering.

Very abruptly.

Ten minutes. That was about as long a period as anyone could work down there in that steadily heating sweat box formed by the face of the fire-retaining bulkhead on one side and a nerve-tearing wall of high explosive on the other. While at the same time you clawed for breath through a fine mist of salt water spray and stumbled blindly, agonizingly, with one monstrous burden after another. On and on and on for ever.

Or for ten minutes, which seemed the same thing. Until a

haggard replacement face loomed beside you in the dim light, and shaking hands helped you clamber dazedly up the projecting myriad of nose cones before they too pulled, and lifted, and stumbled through their own personal eternity of agony . . .

Not that you rested when you finally got out. Because there was a ship on fire somewhere, and there was always some sadistic bastard ready to blink reproachfully through Al Jolson eyes as you collapsed uncaringly in the yellow ochre slush on the deck. So you stared back at your enemy for a brief moment of total exhaustion, really finding out for the first time in your life the true meaning of hatred . . . then you dragged yourself to your feet and snatched the hose jet from him while he reeled away to relieve someone else.

And to hate them too. Just as much as you hated him.

09.45 hrs . . .

Chippie sat down abruptly with a glare of black-bloody-mindedness. 'I'm not doin' another hand's-turn,' he announced defiantly. 'Not till one o' you younger lay-abouts gets off've 'is backside an' gets me a drink o' water . . .'

The Bosun turned his hose on him. The Carpenter blew away in a flailing omelette of spray and outraged, spluttering vituperation.

'Oh, *sorry*, Carpenter,' the Bosun said.

And eyed me sideways. Slyly.

10.20 hrs . . .

Little Apprentice Meehan handed me a tin can brimming with tea. I stared at it disbelievingly for a few seconds before swallowing it convulsively. It tasted like the nectar of the Gods.

All on his own the boy had ventured into the *Maya Star*'s wrecked galley, still containing the dismembered fragments of a chief cook, and rummaged around until he'd rescued a tin of condensed milk and a packet of Jeremy Prethero's favourite Ceylonese *Lapsong Souchong*.

He filled my tin again from a larger billy made out of a metal biscuit box with a looped wire handle. There were bits of ash and charred embers floating in it.

'How did you boil the water?' I asked blankly. 'Gifford said the galley stove was shot up.'

It was only when the youngster smiled that I noticed most of his eyebrows and the front of his hair was all frizzled and burnt.

'Number five hold, Sir,' he giggled. 'I held the can over the fire on a pole. Just like I used to do when I was a boy scout, only in a bigger way.'

10.55 hrs . . .

The sun finally made an appearance.

It wasn't good news. Apart from the tropical heat we could expect from now on, it would also clear the visibility. And there was still a *Kriegsmarine* warship somewhere out there, perhaps steaming towards us right at this minute with eye-straining look-outs closed up and gunners waiting expectantly. Impatiently.

More than likely a bit trigger-happy, after their previous humiliation.

And that worried me too – why they'd left us in the first place – because surely she could have manoeuvred adequately enough on her twin screws to keep us within sight and range until the coup de grâce.

Or had her commander decided we were finished anyway? God knows we must have looked as though we were, but even that conclusion gave me a cold tingle in the pit of my stomach. Because in that case he'd deliberately steamed away in the knowledge that there were – or by rights, should have been – wounded and shocked men threshing under a carpet of oil beside a sinking *Maya Star* . . . which in *its* turn could mean impassive, unhelpful Teutonic faces simply watching as we struggled in the water the next time she tracked us down.

Or maybe they wouldn't be all that impassive. Maybe

65

they'd be full of concentration next time. Gazing through the sights of depressed machine-gun barrels . . .

11.15 hrs . . .
Second Cook Gifford dropped a shell. It landed on its nose with a blood-freezing *crash.*

11.15 hrs and thirty seconds . . .
The last of five cargo dumpers cleared the hold in a flying leap, and that was myself.

But I still overtook Chippie and Cleese before I got to the bottom of the well deck ladder, then slowed for the first time as it penetrated my fogged brain that I hadn't actually heard a bang yet.

We all trooped back towards number six in an uncomfortable embarrassed straggle, like guilty children caught playing truant.

Nobody looked at anybody else. Not for quite a long time.

Nobody spoke to Gifford either. Not for bloody ages!

11.40 hrs . . .
Third Mate Ainslie limped down from his spell of fighting the fires on the boat deck.

'I think we've beaten it up there,' he muttered in a voice which suggested he was past caring either way. 'Stopped it spreading over to the port side.'

He carried on past me and forced his leg over the coaming of number six. I could see his knuckles white with the effort of holding his balance.

'Oh, this FUCKING war . . .' he sobbed with a terrible savagery before he finally lowered himself down to the heat and the humidity and the impossible misery of his next ten minutes in hell.

I didn't tell him that we hadn't beaten number five.

That the blaze buried under there was actually getting worse if anything . . .

66

'C'n I borrow yer hose a minnit, Sir?' Chippie asked. 'There's a bit've rubbish smoking over there by the ladder.'

He swung round clumsily as the force of the jet took over. Bosun Fletcher, luxuriously inhaling his first cigarette since we'd embarked on this crazy escapade, took the stream full bore and finished up like a floundering, cursing starfish in his own personal pool.

'Oh, *sorry*, Bosun,' the Carpenter said.

And eyed me sideways. Slyly.

12.25 hrs . . .

Next to me in the sweat box Bombardier Timmer dragged yet another shell from its stowage, then his hand slipped and he stumbled backwards. He threw his forearm against the bulkhead to steady himself – and snatched it away again with a yelp.

We stared at each other expressionlessly through the dim light with the sweat and the spray dripping unheeded into our eyes and forming white runnels down the dirt coating our hollow, skull-like features.

'I'm sorry,' he panted. 'I just don't know any more. They . . . it could happen any time . . .'

I just smiled vacantly back at him. Like a mindless idiot.

Because it seemed good news at the time. Any prospect of an imminent release from that wretched torment.

12.34 hrs . . .

They dragged me over the coaming and I collapsed beside Timmer uncaringly, staring up towards the blue sky at a mast which loomed high above me at one moment then seemed to topple sideways and over as my vision blurred and I felt the whole world spiralling crazily into a black, limitless void.

Seaman Cleese floated past, trudging towards his ten minutes of purgatory with the look of a man forcing himself to approach the scaffold. His face was grey, the grey of a living corpse. The soulless, ghastly colour of war.

I prayed, 'Please God, let me die now, this minute. Because no human being can suffer as much as I am suffering . . .'

But then my eyes fell on a man slumped against the base of the disconsolately angled gun above me. And he didn't have any colour at all in *his* pain-racked, hopeless expression.

He didn't have a left arm either. Simply a bloody, tattered stump wrapped in a cook's striped apron.

So I climbed back to my feet and went to work again.

Because, one way or another, I knew *my* agony would only to be have endured for a little while longer.

12.40 hrs . . .

Seaman Cleese sagged in a senseless heap to the bottom of the sweat box. We manhandled the inert body on deck and the Bosun looked at me grimly, queryingly. The heat radiatng ithrough that bulkhead was reaching the critical level for survival even without the impossible overload of intense physical effort.

'We stay,' I snarled. 'If I have to put an axe through the soddin' *boats* we stay!'

'I 'ad a feelin' you'd say that,' the Bosun retorted. 'You're as bloody-minded as that Carpenter.'

Then he grinned.

'An' me,' he added. After a quick glance round to make sure Chippie couldn't hear.

13.00 hrs . . .

Apprentice Meehan handed me another tin can full of tea. This time there were brown leaves floating on the surface along with the ash, and he gave an apologetic shrug while I drained it uncaringly.

'Sorry it's not brewed so well, Sir,' he said, 'but I've had a bit of a job finding a decent hot spot to boil the water . . .'

I pushed past him and half ran, half slithered towards the coaming of number five. Ainslie and Second Wireless Operator Martin were apathetically clinging to the hoses, doggedly sweeping the jets from side to side as we'd been doing continuously for the past few hours, covering the area of the gutted hold with the blind, repetitive motions of automatons.

Only now, as each arc of the spray blew the top blanket of fire away and then passed on, there was a momentary lull. And even then only smaller flames appeared, clambering almost unwillingly through the water-saturated mess.

'Don't apologize, son,' I whispered. 'That was the nicest cup of tea I've ever tasted . . .'

13.10 hrs . . .

Able Seaman Toomey flopped over the coaming after his ten minute martyrdom and blinked up at me through red-rimmed eyes. I saw his hands were bound with strips of filthy rag while his cracked lips moved with difficulty.

'They're too hot,' he croaked. 'The bloody things're gettin' too hot to touch.'

I watched numbly as he pulled himself to the bulwarks, leaning out over the sea, trying desperately to catch even a catspaw of breeze to cool his parboiled features. Then the winch clattered yet again and another blackly evil monstrosity swung out of the hold, jerked across the deck under the snatch of the runner and came to an abrupt halt, penduluming and rotating slowly above the sea and clear of the ship's side.

'Cod end, Mister B,' Chippie cued sharply from behind the winch. I started out of my reverie, muttered a resentful 'Sorry', and jerked at the net release line in my hand.

The shell fell through the mesh, turning end over end below the level of the rail.

It exploded as it hit the surface, slamming a great feathering gout of water high in the air to splatter shockingly back across the deck and our startled, whirling figures.

'*Christl*' Cleese squealed, not looking at all somnolent any more.

Toomey hadn't moved, still leaning over the capping of the bulwark as if he hadn't even noticed the detonation below him. I forced my legs to stop their involuntary trembling and walked over to him, feeling every pair of eyes on deck following me hypnotically.

'Toomey,' I said tremulously.

He didn't answer. Didn't even lift his head fractionally. I touched his shoulder with a tentative finger.

Able Seaman Toomey crumpled sideways and collapsed on his back in the scuppers. One eye stared up at me with an all-too-familiar and astonished gaze.

He didn't have a second eye. Only an obscenely flowering cavity where the shell splinter had entered . . .

It seemed very unfair, Toomey dying when he did and after all that effort.

Less than twenty minutes later Third Mate Ainslie came up out of number six hold and stood beside me as I played my hose on the last stubbornly-resisting area of flame along the port side of five.

Our fire break was complete. Two lashed sprayers were now pouring a constantly cooling stream against the protective tarpaulin hung across the exposed face of the ammunition, and while there was every possibility that the temporarily subdued remnants of the blaze on the other side of that tortured bulkhead might well break out once again – and most certainly would continue to radiate heat for hours, even days – at least we had a breathing space. Or most of us. Apart from Toomey . . .

'We've finished,' the Third muttered in a faint tone of wonderment. 'Would you believe we've actually *finished* the job?'

I wasn't able to react for a moment, still only capable of concentrating what little mental reserves I had left on the major task of directing a fire hose.

Until, gradually, the impact of his words sank in.

I frowned, lifting my gaze to the bulk of the *Maya Star*'s mutilated superstructure. Laboriously I began to assess the precise nature of the situation which I, thirteen other seamen and one irrepressibly resolute soldier now found ourselves in . . .

. . . aboard a gutted, defenceless half-ship some two hundred miles off a jungle-infested and largely uninhabited coastline. And in the middle of a war.

With no compass, charts or navigational information; no efficient means of steering other than a ponderous emergency position aft – even if we knew *which* course to steer in the first place . . . No medical assistance for our wounded; no wireless with which to call for help, no certainty that our dormant fire would stay dormant for very long . . . no absolute certainty, for that matter, that our high explosive cargo still couldn't simply trigger-off in one instantaneous sear of expanding fire . . .

In fact only one factor *was* indisputable – that there was an enemy warship somewhere out there – a very frustrated enemy warship, which could be returning to search for us at this precise moment. Methodically hunting us down even as we drifted . . .

The tropical sun was very hot but suddenly I shivered.

'No, Three Oh,' I said as levelly as I could, '. . . I'm afraid we've only just started.'

5

So now it was simply a question of priorities. The only problem was – how did I decide which priority took precedence over all the other priorities . . .

Obviously we had to get the *Maya Star* under way again as quickly as possible, both to evacuate the immediate area in case that damned raider did return to finish the job and, almost as urgently, to seek medical aid for our wounded.

Only that, in its turn, raised several other grim spectres. For a start I wasn't even certain of our precise position now, not after several hours of aimless drifting. Even if I had been I still couldn't lay off a course to head for anywhere in particular, with or without a compass to steer by. Oh, we'd certainly raise a landfall, I wasn't such an incompetent navigator as all that, and there was plenty of it available in that the whole of South America lay about two hundred miles away over there.

But the trouble was that the Amazon basin covered an area larger than central Europe and was either uninhabited, unexplored or plain bloody undesirable. Hospitals . . . ? We'd be lucky even to find a primitive coastal settlement, with or without friendly natives.

Which, in its unavoidable turn, presented yet another grisly prospect – Steward Thomson's mutilated arm. Because I didn't need a doctor to tell me that Thomson couldn't survive long enough to reach expert help and sterile operating conditions – not even the basic requirement of an anaesthetic, for that matter. Coldly I realized that Gifford was right, and that we would have to trim that ragged stump within the next few hours. Then seal it somehow. Before tropical gangrene set in and killed Steward

Thomson anyway, after a screaming, mindless limbo of agony.

But only when we were steaming again. With *some* hope for an end to this nightmare voyage . . .

The emergency after-steering position was controlled from a small pedestal situated on the poop, forward of the more recently added gun and connected to the steering engine in the tiller flat below through a series of rods and bevel wheels. Hopefully – apart from the obvious fact that a complete two-spoke section of the teak wheel had been shot away during the raider's last salvo – the rest of the system appeared undamaged.

I left the Third Mate and Sparks to test the gear while Gifford and Bombardier Timmer returned to the unhappily neglected task of treating the injured. Chippie led a weary, sweating straggle on a preliminary search of the burned-out upper deck as Bosun Fletcher and myself headed for the engine room and Archie Nolan.

We took Greaser Hotchkiss with us, the invariably voluble engineering rating having recovered from his blast-induced shock in time to work like a Trojan along with the rest of us in number six, accompanying his labours with a constant and darkly muttered flow of '. . . bloody Jerries . . . bloody mad sodgers . . . bloody Navy routing . . . bloody lousy bloody *luck* . . .'

'Bloody shut UP, 'Otchkiss!' the Bosun had finally snarled.

'. . . bloody *Bo*suns . . .' Hotchkiss had continued. Discreetly.

I hesitated before I reached the main deck, glancing back over our battleground of the past few hours. Now only Cleese and young Apprentice Meehan remained on stand-by beside the charred maw of five, constantly wreathed in a clinging fog of smoke and steam. Everywhere lay a wreckage-strewn desolation of twisted steel and eviscerated cargo and the forlornly hanging wires of scarred derricks.

From above I caught the hushed muttering of voices as Chippie's crowd ventured uneasily into the gutted accommodation where so many of our shipmates still slept – and that reminded me of another problem. Involuntarily I felt my eyes drawn to the pathetic strip of canvas covering the starboard scuppers. Three and a half pairs of feet protruded from under. We hadn't been able to recover all the remains of Bombardier Timmer's small fighting force . . .

. . . and that clawed me back to the question of priorities again. Because this *was* the tropics. Where, under certain circumstances, the dead demanded even more immediate attention than the living.

'*Damn*!' I swore softly, but with an awful despair.

'Sir?'

'The dead. We'll have to bury them very soon . . . and we haven't even got a bloody Bible.'

The Second Engineer was half-propped, half-lying outside the engine room entrance when we arrived. He looked at us anxiously and I could see the question in his eyes, behind the pain.

'All clear in six, Archie,' I called reassuringly. 'For the moment, anyway.'

He relaxed visibly, then made a wry, apologetic gesture. 'I got scared. Down below, all by myself, an' then the explosion . . .'

'Toomey. One premature went off and he caught a splinter . . .' I stopped, trying to assess the extent of his burns and feeling a bit guilty while I did so, because it wasn't simply compassion for Nolan's agony – he also happened to be the only engineer we had left and, together with the muttering Greaser Hotchkiss, was our sole hope if anything went wrong mechanically between here and . . . well . . . and South America. Or thereabouts.

'I'm heading inshore for assistance, Archie. Can you cope down below. Along with Hotchkiss here?'

He tried to smile but the pain dragged his mouth into a wry grimace. 'Do I have a choice?'

'Not now,' Fletcher threatened cheerfully. 'Not after us ditchin' all them shells so's you could travel first class, you don't.'

The Second staggered when we helped him to his feet and I caught the glint of suppuration already evident on his burned shoulder. This time there was no ulterior motive behind the sympathy I felt.

'We'll rig you a cot down there, soon as we can,' I said. 'You don't need to climb the ladders if you don't want to. I'll have your vittles sent down.'

'I'll stay with yer, Sir,' Greaser Hotchkiss promised generously. 'Both've us together, like moles in an 'ole. An' I'll keep talkin' so's yer won't weary . . .'

'I . . . er . . . I'll get down and start her up,' Nolan said hurriedly while, this time, even the Bosun looked sympathetic at the awful prospect now facing the Second, incarcerated for hours with the most garrulous man aboard the *Maya Star*.

'Oh well,' he sniffed philosophically as the black gang disappeared haltingly below. 'Mister Nolan's still better off than me, even now. Because I gotter put up wi' that bloody ignorant old Carpenter. An' that's *real* sufferin', whatever way you look at it.'

Chippie met us as we climbed to the boat deck. His normally florid face looked noticeably paler, even a little older.

'We're still searchin', Sir. But we found some. Quite a lot of them was still in their berths . . .'

I remember standing up there on that splintered open deck, in the twisted shadow of the *Maya Star*'s once-proud funnel, with the sea all around a sparkling deep blue under the now clear tropical sky. And the Bosun and the Carpenter came and stood silently beside me while the rest of the crowd – tired, dishevelled and filthy – grouped together in

75

an almost protective semi-circle around the things which had been placed gently in the shade of the deckhousing.

Only they weren't *things*, those shrivelled black monkey objects. They'd been men, shipmates and friends, until a very short time ago. Until a clandestine ship masquerading under an inoffensive flag came by, and brought an almost insignificant bit of the war into our home.

'I'll sew them up, Sir,' Chippie said quietly. 'All proud an' neat an' ship-shape.'

I blinked and turned away. 'I'll be on the bridge,' I heard myself say. 'Looking for the captain.'

We recovered poor Jeremy Prethero ourselves, the Bosun and I. Working side by side under the hot sun with tightly clenched lips and the taste of green bile ever at the back of our throats. But it was something that I, for my part, knew I had to do – to be involved in personally – as a mark of respect for the late master of the *Maya Star*.

I did hope Mrs Prethero would have approved. Just this once . . .

And then the two of us leaned for a few silent moments on what remained of the bridge rail, simply staring out over the sea and thinking our own private thoughts while the ship moved sullenly on the flat swell, warningly almost, as if anxious to be off and away from this area of sudden violence.

'They're out there still,' Bosun Fletcher muttered, reading the ship's uneasiness with the indefinable *rapporte* that only a seaman could understand.

'Jerrie?'

'Aye. They're out there somewhere . . . She c'n sense it.'

I looked, but I couldn't see anything. Only a distant, unbroken horizon with the blue of the sea dissolving imperceptibly into the lighter opacity of the sky. Nothing there, not a splinter that could be a mast or even the almost indetectable haze that might indicate a diesel vessel masked by the earth's curve.

But it didn't mean anything, and I couldn't stop that

chill of apprehension from creeping up my spine again. Because I knew, and the old Bosun knew, that the ship was frightened.

And we also knew that a ship, when it felt like that, could never be wrong.

Ainslie met me at the break of the poop as I returned aft. He was looking very pleased with himself and I couldn't help feeling a little more hopeful when I saw the beam on what had previously been a rather downcast face.

'Steering checks out O.K.,' he said. 'And we've established communication with the engine room. Nolan's ready to go when you give the word, Sir.'

I frowned absently. Certainly that was one of the less pressing problems that had hung at the back of my mind, anyway – the question of relaying engine movement orders from what was now the ship's control position aft all the way to midships and then sixty or seventy feet down through the racketing, roaring bedlam of sound which was our engine room. Even forming a chain to pass verbal instructions would tax our limited manpower to the limit, without considering all the other functions necessary once we began to manoeuvre in restricted inshore waters.

If we ever managed to get as far as those inshore waters, in the first place, that was.

'How?' I asked doubtfully. The Third Mate winked at Sparks and they both grinned cleverly.

'Dial an engineer. By kind permission of the United States Army an' the Ministry of Supply.'

'Don't bugger about,' I retorted irritably. 'How the hell do you find a telephone in the middle of the South Atlantic? There's absolutely nothing in the middle of the South Atlantic.'

'Except Jerrie raiders,' the Bosun inserted gloomily.

'Number four upper tween decks, Sir. Don't you remember we loaded three cases of military field sets? I broke 'em out and looked. There must've been fifty, sixty phones altogether.'

'And we know there's enough wire – most've it's lying around the well deck.' I couldn't help grinning myself. It was only a modest stroke of fortune but it was something. A very small victory.

'We calculated roughly. Around two thousand miles of it, give or take a drum or two. Nearly enough to phone home.'

'Ask 'em to send us a few things,' I said. 'Like maybe three cruisers and a compass.'

Ainslie stopped smiling and scratched his head. 'And that's another problem, isn't it?'

I shrugged. 'Actually there's not a lot to be gained by being too accurate. We know where Brazil lies, and without charts any landfall we make has to be a pure guess anyway ... When we begin steaming, the sun and stars'll be enough to get us to first base. After that we can decide on our next move ...'

Suddenly the deck beneath our feet stirred, then settled into a steady, resonant vibration while the empty brass cartridge cases littering the poop began to clink and rattle excitedly. I looked up at the centrecastle, the torn funnel was again wreathed in a faint blue haze of exhaust.

'At least we've got engines,' Sparks remarked cynically, as if he wasn't expecting anything else to go right for us after all that had happened.

There was a blood-freezing shriek from behind and I swivelled nervously, shying away. 'The telephone, Sir,' Ainslie said, straight-faced. 'They're the kind you whizz the handle to generate a current.'

I picked it up. My hand was still shaking and I wondered bleakly how I'd stand up to a real crisis now. 'Bridge – Belay that . . . poop deck here. Mate speaking.'

Nolan's voice sounded a long way off, barely discernible above the background clamour of the engine room. 'Captain,' he shouted metallically. 'You're the captain now,

78

remember? Ready to go when you are.'

'Aye, aye. But keep her at revolutions for ten knots, Archie. I don't want to risk fanning a new blaze in five hold right now.'

I dropped the handset back in the green painted case and even as I did so felt the deck begin to throb more urgently, bringing an almost exhilarating sense of life back into what had been for too long a dead ship, Slowly I could see the high boat deck starting to swing across the sky as we gathered way while, behind me, the torn Red Ensign over the taffrail stirred into little restless flutters.

'Steer as close to nor' west as you can, Mister Ainslie,' I called. He hesitated with his hands on the wheel.

'Shouldn't we be heading in a more southerly direction, Sir. Sou' west say, for the land?'

He was right, of course. But then again he hadn't been on the bridge a few minutes ago, that time when the ship spoke to the Bosun and me, and gave us her intangible warning.

'If you were a German raider captain and you wanted to make an interception again, just to make sure of us – what would you do first?'

'Probably lay off our likely course towards help, then . . .' His face suddenly cleared and he looked a bit embarrassed. 'Sorry. You mean to run parallel to the coast for a while before heading in. So's Jerrie can't possibly anticipate our final track.'

'Crafty Captin,' the Bosun grinned approvingly. 'Sneaky, like yon Eytalian feller in the olden days. Mac whatsit.'

'Machiavelli?' Sparks offered.

'Aye, that wus him,' Fletcher nodded. 'Mac Avellee.'

I didn't answer. I didn't feel particularly clever either. Because I still had that premonition of impending threat, just like the ship had.

And all the tactical subterfuge in the world wouldn't help us then. Not if I was right.

'I'm plannin' to do somethin' with Thomson's arm in about

79

an hour, Cap'n, if that's O.K. with you?'

I swallowed nervously – *It* being O.K. with Steward Thomson seemed to be rather more to the point right then. But, 'Why an hour, Gifford. Why not right away?'

As usual he didn't smile, he simply gestured over to where the Steward lay propped against the bulkhead. Bombardier Timmer was kneeling beside him, stubbornly holding something to the bloodless lips.

'It'll take that long f'r the anaesthetic to work properly,' Gifford retorted. 'Two bottles should do the trick. An' that's all I could find in the saloon.'

I looked at the whisky. It was a very good brand and I thought two whole bottles would be about right. Especially seeing Steward Thomson had always been a teetotaller.

Until now.

'What about the other two? How bad are they?'

For the first time Gifford seemed a little uncertain. Obviously he was out of his depth with Thomson's appalling wound, but so far he'd always given the impression of being able to cope – so long as shock or infection could be kept at bay. While the two head wounds were bad, they probably looked a lot worse than they were. So why did the Second Cook seem so doubtful?

'I dunno. Lamps should be O.K. Half 'is scalp's been tore off but it's still mostly superficial. As long as he rests up 'e'll probably be none the worse in a few days – apart from lookin' like Custer after the battle . . . but Sproat's different. Sort of odd some'ow, like he's not all there any more.'

'Concussion? That can make people act a bit strangely.'

He shrugged. 'Maybe. But I'd guess it's worse than that. I think the wound's through the skull, maybe a bit've shell splinter still in there.'

'Oh Christ,' I thought helplessly. Then I walked over to where the two injured men lay and forced a reassuring smile.

'Not long now. We'll be heading inshore in a few hours,

then with a bit of luck it'll be clean sheets and pretty Brazilian nurses all round.'

The Lamptrimmer squinted up at me, looking all lopsided, one eye masked under a bloodstained blue and white turban and face the same drained pallor as the wounded Thomson's. He still tried a grin, though, despite his misery.

'I'm quite 'appy ter settle f'r even an ugly one, Mister B... Soon as I gets shut of this 'eadache.'

I turned to the man beside him. 'Sproat ... Blonde or brunette?'

But the seaman didn't react at all. He simply lay there staring blankly up at me – through me, almost – then, even as I watched, something happened in those dull, unblinking eyes which caused me to start back in involuntary horror with the shock of it.

Because for one brief moment it was as if a dark curtain had parted deep in the recesses of Sproat's mind. Oh, only fleetingly, like the blink of a high speed camera shutter ... yet in that one chilling glimpse alone I felt I had encroached, somehow, into the most secret hiding place of a man ...

And found myself looking on stark, unfettered madness.

Gifford was watching me closely. 'You seen it too, didn't you?'

I nodded shakily. 'God help him if there's any permanent damage to the brain.'

The Second Cook eyed the big seaman grimly. 'God help *us*, you mean ... if 'e gets his strength back.'

There was a wind blowing across the *Maya Star*'s decks again when I passed Cleese and Meehan, still patiently spraying the charred jumble of number five. I stopped and looked critically over the buckled coaming, noticing the way little whorls from the ten knot breeze we were now creating left brightly glowing embers in their passing.

'There's a helluva heat still comin' through,' Cleese muttered uneasily. 'Been like that ever since we got under way, jus' creeping back up to the top like it's trying to break out again.'

I walked back to six and stared bleakly at the serrated rows of high explosive. A fine mist of spray curled back over the canvas shield, drawn skywards by the slight suction created under the ship's momentum. Wearily I swung my leg on to the ladder and clambered down to the dimly lit space we'd cleared to ventilate our lethal cargo. The bulkhead was twinkling under a steady waterfall from the hoses but if you looked very carefully you could just detect the faint miasma of steam wisping from its surface.

I placed my hand tentatively on a random nose cone – it was warm, but not as warm as the one which had killed Able Seaman Toomey. He'd had to protect his hands just before he died, and this next tier wasn't that hot.

Yet.

But I still had a nasty intuition that we hadn't finished with the fire in the *Maya Star*'s belly. Not by a long chalk.

'What d'you reckon, Captain?' Cleese called anxiously, framed as a black silhouette against the square of blue sky above me. I got up and climbed to the deck thoughtfully.

'If the fire breaks through, let me know immediately,' I said. 'We can always stop the ship and cut down the windage again. As long as those bloody shells don't get any hotter than they are.'

Cleese reassured me fervently. 'Don't you worry, Sir. I'll keep checking an' shout loud an' clear if they do.'

I didn't comment as I left them and headed for the bridge.

If he fell down on the job we'd probably all find out at precisely the same blinding micro-second . . .

Chippie looked up as I walked towards him along the boat deck. Several canvas-wrapped forms lay patiently waiting in a neat line along the strip of shade formed by the deck house. Some of them seemed very small, not at all like men, and he shrugged awkwardly, almost apologetically, when he caught the startled frown I must have betrayed.

'Aye, they're only little – the badly burned ones,' he said, and then he hesitated, toying reflectively with the shiny sailmaker's needle gripped in his horny hand. I wondered if he hadn't had enough. Preparing our dead for burial wasn't a job for one man alone, not even when he'd insisted on doing things his way.

'You've done a lot of them really proud, Chippie,' I suggested gently. 'Why not let someone else take a spell for a change?'

He shook his head and the white hair seemed saintly somehow, matted and dirty though it was from the fires in the ship.

'I sewn up a lot o' shipmates in me time. I learned how when I wus a lad under sail, Mister Barton, an' I allus reckoned it wus a sort o' duty, part of the price a man has ter pay when 'e goes to sea . . .'

He ground to a halt but I could see there was something still bothering him. 'Only . . . what?' I coaxed softly.

The old man glared up at me bitterly. 'It's a tradition an' a kindness. Always to put the last stitch through the nose, Mister – jus' to make sure the poor devil really *has* parted 'is cable, don't ye see? But I can't, dammit . . . not wi' the badly burned lads I can't!'

I'm sure I blanched. I must have done. But this time he didn't let on if he'd noticed.

'I don't think they'll mind,' I heard myself say from a distance. 'I really don't think any of them will mind at all . . .'

We'd been under way for a good half hour by the time I actually reached my original goal – the *Maya Star*'s wrecked bridge. And after having spent most of that period listening to either an apprehensive fire watcher, a pessimistic amateur surgeon-elect or a macabrely frustrated under- taker I'd lost every glimmer of the hopeful euphoria I'd felt when we'd first begun to steam again. In fact now I was virtually resigned to a permanent state of nervous anticipation, simply waiting for the next crisis to beckon with spine-chilling certainty.

But at least it meant that only the nature of the emergency would come as a surprise from now on.

And naturally, as I'd gloomily predicted, it didn't take very long to find the answer to *that* particular riddle either . . .

Able Seaman Ricketts saw it first. Only about a mile ahead and lying right across our track . . .

We'd made a good start on clearing the tangled mass of debris, most of it having to be levered and toppled over the forward face of the centrecastle to tumble forty feet to the deck below. I hadn't risked dumping any wreckage directly over the side – if our raider chanced to sight any traces of our passing they would have acted as an unmistakable signpost in the calm sea, a total betrayal of my intention to head nor' west before actually closing the coast.

But as I'd feared, pretty well anything which might have been of some help in pinpointing our prospective landfall had been destroyed. Among the scrambled ruins originally forming the wheelhouse itself we found only one pair of still-serviceable binoculars, two pencils, the helmsman's course board still bearing the chalked scrawl of dead Fourth Mate Gulliver and a crushed tin box containing the remains of the night watchkeepers' sandwiches. Everything else – telemotor steering pedestal, engine telegraphs, barograph, clock – had been either compacted into unrecognizable scrap or, in the case of the binnacle, sheared in two as if by some gigantic cleaver.

We did find the compass bowl. The glass face was, remarkably, still undamaged but when I turned it over I found the pressure-compensating diaphragm buckled and useless, and there was a great silvery bubble in the liquid. I kept it, but only because it might be of some help in maintaining a straight course. As an instrument it would be totally inaccurate anyway, re-sited so far aft without any correction for magnetic deviation.

As far as the chartroom was concerned our chances of salvaging anything were virtually nil from the start. Fire had totally ravaged the larger part of what had already been converted to matchwood by the raider's opening salvo. Sextants, chronometer, Admiralty pilots and sailing directions, almanacs, tables . . . all gone, burned to ashes or melted into misshapen, mocking blobs which had finally tumbled through the skeletal ribs of the deck and into Jeremy Prethero's gutted cabin below.

Though we did find one item which, for one exhilarating moment, helped to raise my flagging spirits − one chart folio from the ship's stock. One possibly priceless wad of information relating to some part of the world where the *Maya Star* had previously been.

I leafed through the charred sheets, hopefully devouring the printed legends in the bottom right hand corners. And certainly we *had* covered that part of the globe, and hoped to once again. But not right away, not in this current voyage, while the contents of that particular folio wouldn't really tell me a lot about the dangers offered by the South American coastline . . .

Not in *Chart Number 2675 English Channel, eastern portion.* Or in *Chart 3337 − River Thames, London Bridge to Woolwich.* Or *Chart 2693 Approaches to Felixstowe, Harwich and Ipswich with the Rivers Stour, Orwell and Deben . . . Chart Number* bloody *1406 − Dover to Orfordness . . .*

. . . but then Able Seaman Ricketts had blurted excitedly, 'Somethin' in the water. Dead ahead!' and I was slipping and staggering over the remaining jumble with our one surviving pair of glasses in my hand and that old familiar tingle down my spine.

Even magnified by the 7 x 50 Barr and Strouds there was no indication of what that anonymous, low-lying object could be, not at first. It was quite small, I could make that much out, and almost level with the glassy surface which accounted for our not having raised it until we were fairly close.

The apprehension slowly subsided as I screwed my eyes into the glasses, trying to make out detail. Whatever it was it didn't seem dangerous and that was the most important thing. While this *was* an area somewhere off the mouth of one of the largest rivers in the world – all forms of flotsam could be carried miles out to sea on the fanning currents of the Amazon delta.

Until . . .

'It's a *boat*,' I snapped suddenly as the indeterminate blob in the water finally resolved into a recognizable form. 'Some sort of waterlogged boat . . .'

Eventually we closed the mysterious craft, but not without difficulty. Conning a ship of the *Maya Star*'s size, with the view forward masked from the poop by the bulk of the centrecastle, was a bit like driving a motor car and using only the side windows for vision, so I had to manoeuvre from my vantage point on the bridge, passing movement orders aft through a straggling line of seamen, and made a mental resolution to borrow another few lengths of the War Department's two thousand mile would-be land link to make life a little easier at sea.

Ainslie and Bosun Fletcher were waiting for me on the well deck as I slid hurriedly down the ladders after stopping engines. Together we craned out over the low bulwarks, trying to make sense of the enigmatic relic now lying alongside.

It *was* an open boat, about thirty feet long and so badly damaged it had foundered until the sea lapped and gurgled over the thwarts themselves. It looked very familiar in many ways and I knew I'd seen the type many times before. In fact I could see two more almost identical twins right now if I raised my eyes to the level of our own boat deck.

It was a standard merchant ship's lifeboat. Even more disturbingly – a British merchantman's lifeboat . . . and it certainly couldn't have belonged to the *Maya Star*.

Someone else had been in bad trouble in this immediate area, and not very long ago. The weather prior to our own attack by the raider had been too violent to have allowed that splintered craft to remain afloat, held up only by the minimal buoyancy of its few remaining thwart tanks.

Even the damage looked familiar, the way the shell splinters had ripped and torn great gashes through the wooden hull. And then I really went cold inside as I stared grimly down at that forlorn legacy of what had obviously been an enemy warship's passing.

Because there was quite a lot of neat holes punched through the bows of the waterlogged boat. Little holes, evenly spaced. Just like the bullet holes a vectoring machine gun makes . . .

'There's no one *in* it,' the Third Mate said. Hopefully.

'Yeah,' Fletcher retorted ominously. 'But that don't mean there never was. *Before* the bastards started shooting!'

We couldn't make out any name painted on the sub-merged bow, it was too badly scarred. But the shimmering black letters seen through the water around the stern did confirm one thing. That, whoever she'd been until a few hours ago, she'd originally been a ship registered in the port of Liverpool – just like ourselves.

Which only left one major question to answer. But that posed probably the most chilling riddle of all . . . whether that anonymous sister-casualty had met up with what could only have been the same German surface raider before, or *after*, our own abortive escape of the early morning.

Fletcher managed to frame my unspoken fears with his usual succint directness.

'If them poor devils have bumped into Jerrie since we wus in action ourselves, gents,' he pronounced with almost funeral relish, 'then we aren't runnin' away at all . . .

87

We're *chasin*' the bastards instead.'

There were two more tasks to face in my list of priorities, and I didn't know which prospect appalled me the most – the preservation of the living, or the disposal of the dead. I decided that the operation to Steward Thomson's arm must come first. I didn't think those still, silent parcels on the boat deck would mind waiting just a little longer, and it seemed important that they should go to their final port of destination in a respectful, leisurely way, unhurried by the hour-to-hour pressures of survival demanded by the still alive.

Second Cook Gifford had already prepared his operating theatre with the conscientious attention to detail that any master chef would apply to the planning of an efficient galley. The saloon table had been scrubbed and there were wide holes drilled at each corner in order to lash the unfortunate amputee securely in place. As the entire midships lighting system had been rendered unserviceable he'd taken a direct lead to the engine room below and rigged two enormous cargo lamps above the table. I hoped he'd also been as meticulous with the blackout curtaining. The tropical night would shutter down like a high speed blanket shortly and I wanted the *Maya Star* dark.

Dark and secret, hidden in our own black world. Our frightened, furtive, wartime world.

And then there were the instruments, all twinkling and neat under the glare of the floodlights. Gifford had scoured the ship with a terrible ingenuity to produce the tools of his self-appointed and, I prayed, very temporary profession. A selection of well-honed boning knives from the demolished galley, a pair of scissors resurrected from Able Seaman Cleese's covertly-stowed embroidery kit, chisels from the Carpenter's tool box . . . sailmaker's needles already threaded with gut . . .

'Gut?' I queried blankly. 'Howd'you find gut aboard a ship, Gifford?'

'Your cabin,' he retorted unashamedly. 'It's still not too badly burned out an' I remembered you wus a fisherman f'r a hobby.'

'Oh!' I said faintly. I'd forgotten I'd ever had a hobby. I'd even forgotten I had a cabin. And a bunk. I picked up a hacksaw with macabre curiosity, the blade had been heated and looked much smoother than usual.

'Engineers' store,' he offered, looking a bit pleased with himself compared with his usual dead-pan impression of truculence. 'When they give it to me it wus toothed rough enough to saw through the funnel, an' that'd just tear through the bone, splinter it like.'

I nodded, swallowing uncomfortably.

'So I got Hotchkiss ter heat the blade, then bash it flat an' re-temper it. It'll do lovely now.'

Timmer and, rather surprisingly, young Radio Operator Martin brought Thomson in, then laid him gently on the table. He was barely conscious and I could see from the fuddled look in his eyes that he didn't know what was happening to him. The whisky seemed to have virtually numbed his nervous system, presumably continuing to act as a buffer to the pain after the initial shock of the wound began to wear off. I didn't think it would do more than help a little, though. Not after Gifford had picked up that hack-saw.

. . . yet it did seem to. Almost as soon as Gifford began to trim the ragged wound Steward Thomson thrashed briefly, then slipped mercifully into a pain- and alcohol-induced oblivion which also made it much easier for us to bear. Yet when I did steal a furtive glance towards the gunner and the wireless man I couldn't detect any outward sign of the nausea I had felt initially – simply an infinite compassion, etched under the glare from the overhead cargo lamps, for the poor wretch lashed to the table.

Twenty minutes later it was nearly over and I had learned to develop ungrudging respect for the tough little ship's cook who – in an atmosphere more akin to the fighting deck of a Napoleonic man o' war stricken in action than a modern day cargo vessel – had worked with such deft competence.

'Just gotter take that flap I left,' Gifford muttered with enormous concentration, 'then stitch it back over the stump like the parson's nose of a chicken . . . an' that's it.'

Silently I passed him the most sophisticated aid we had aboard – a carton of boracic powder from the engine room emergency kit. He sprinkled it liberally over the wound and began to sew with my favourite five-pound breaking strain trout line.

There wasn't any more I could do. 'I'd better get aft again,' I said hesitantly. 'It's after sunset and we're due to alter towards the land now.'

Gifford didn't answer. Just kept stitching neatly and precisely. I wondered if he'd guessed my secondary reason for going. A shamefully selfish one – in that I didn't want to be near that saloon when Steward Thomson began to wake up.

'Thanks, Chef,' I added from the door. Then I just had to ask the question which had niggled consistently at the back of my mind since he'd first started. 'You ever work in a hospital, Gifford? Before you were a cook.'

He stopped sewing for a moment then, and glanced over at me with a sardonic contempt. '*My* old man wus a skin-flint drunk, Mister. He made me get a job soon as I lef' school so's I could keep 'im in beer – until I couldn't stand it no more an' ran away to sea . . .'

'Job?'

And slowly his tight mouth curled into a very faint smile. For the first time ever I actually saw Second Cook Gifford show a spark of humour.

'As a meat boner, Captain . . . in a butcher's shop.'

Steward Thomson had begun to claw his horrific way through the mists of returning consciousness before I got as far as the poop. Even as I passed Ricketts and Deckie Sullivan – still spraying water into number five with the dull glow of the somnolent fire reflecting their startled expressions – I could hear the plaintive animal whimpers carrying from the accommodation.

The darkness had already closed protectively around the *Maya Star* and Ainslie's face hovered as a pale blob at the head of the ladder.

'Thomson?' he asked in a shocked whisper.

'He's coming back to reality now,' I grated. Then I swung away and smashed my fist violently against the barrel of that bloody evil gun.

'DAMN the war!' I snarled for maybe the twentieth occasion on that appalling day. Only this time it really was different.

Because this time it wasn't for myself at all.

I slept for two hours during the night. A nightmare-plagued limbo of hideously burned dead men still walking the decks of some lost, eternally-voyaging ghost ship. While the ship itself sailed erratically across a blood red sea towards a landfall which didn't exist other than in the prayers of a pathetically inadequate captain . . .

Until I slammed bolt upright, with the sweat soaking into the lifejacket I'd used as a pillow and the wild eyes of some haggard, terrified caricature of myself staring from the cracked mirror beside my bunk.

It was still dark. I lit a cigarette with shaking hands and went on deck. It was time to bury our dead, and not only for their own peace but also for the sake of the ship, because a ship feels these things and the *Maya Star* had already suffered an agony of violation. Now I had to try to ease that burden, because I'd had a dream which told me so.

The dawn had come by the time we were all gathered together on the after deck, and the ship had whispered to a temporary halt on the surface of a gentle sea. I remember looking out over the silhouettes of those silent, bare-headed men towards the far horizon and, even as I watched, the tip of the sun's periphery began to climb through the bright, shimmering haze that marked the edge of the world, reaching out with golden fingers to touch the torn Red Ensign covering the body of Captain Jeremy Prethero, Master of the *Maya Star*.

I don't remember what I said over that long, dreadful line of neatly-parcelled shipmates. I know I must have said it badly, with a hesitant, untutored banality made even more inept without the aid of a bible. But at least I did mumble those forlorn phrases with all the sadness a man could ever feel, and the real requiem for the *Maya Star*'s dead sailormen was evinced in the sorrowing eyes of the still living.

And after I had finished, stumbling eventually to an uncertain halt, and just looking pleadingly at Chippie and Bosun Fletcher beside the flag-draped hatch board, I couldn't help but notice the understanding glance that passed between them, and felt pathetically grateful as they lifted the end of the bier, consigning the first body to eternal rest.

And the next . . . And the next . . . Each weighted canvas shape entering with a distant splash to fade towards the bottom of the sea, with only a twinkling, silvery trail of bubbles as a very temporary marker of their going.

Until someone at the back of the crowd called a simple 'Fair weather f'r your voyage, lads.'

And that was . . . well . . . that.

For the moment.

Not that anything did happen for the rest of that sweltering, uneasy morning. Either good or bad.

We constantly watched that distant horizon in the half-hope, half-fear of sighting another ship, but we didn't. We constantly laboured with the hoses going full bore and the bilge pumps spewing a steady stream of black water in our wake, to try to extinguish for once and for all the fire slumbering ominously in number five. But we didn't.

Some of us tried to sleep. But they didn't, not in the end. You would see them a short while later, leaning heavily against the rails and looking just as exhausted as ever and you knew they'd had their own personal nightmares too, and that the ship still steamed in the shadow of dreadful things even after her part crew of cadavers had left her.

We tried to coax a glimmer of response from the quietly mad seaman Sproat. But we couldn't.

We even tried to stop the Bosun and the Carpenter arguing, while at the same time Second Engineer Nolan was trying to stop Greaser Hotchkiss from chatting both incessantly and cheerily above the roar of those hammering engines. But we couldn't. None of us.

But admittedly one thing *did* go right for *someone* aboard.

It was just after midday, while the Third Mate and myself were dubiously trying to calculate our approximate position by estimating longitude from the time differences in sunrise and sunset and work out a latitude based on the altitude of the sun when on the meridian. Which, naturally, we couldn't, not with any certainty. Just like everyone else aboard the bloody ship.

Anyway, the irrepressible Bombardier Timmer had suddenly come dashing after us with a look of utter rapture, yelling, 'Sir! Sir . . . I've managed to fix it, Sir. Only the gearing was damaged an' I've rigged a spare . . . It's O.K. again, Sir!'

I couldn't help feeling a surge of hope. *Anything* had to be good news, a boost to my sadly flagging morale.

'Good lad, Bombardier. Fixed what?'

He took a deep breath before he answered, as if savouring every moment of revelation, almost like a kid giving a very special birthday present.

'The GUN, Sir . . . I've repaired the *gun*!'

I had to turn away without speaking. But I didn't want him to see the tears of disappointment in my eyes.

Around two in the afternoon the wind began to rise, gusting

to maybe fifteen knots from the direction of the land. The passive embers in number five stopped being quite so passive and, fed by the steadily increasing draught, started to glow an incandescent red while the volume of smoke rose to a continual acrid cloud pouring aft across the helm party on the poop.

I watched the growing threat uneasily. I knew we were on the verge of a second major conflagration and the only effective method of controlling it would be to stop the ship, or at least reduce the way on her and lie across the wind to ease the problem. We added another two hose jets and decided to keep on going for a little while longer.

Slightly before four-o-clock in the afternoon Cleese, staring tightly ahead from the bridge, sighted a low, dark patch on the horizon. By half past four it was just possible to make out the peaks of mountains and I knew, without any doubt, that we were finally closing the coast of Brazil.

Well . . . most certainly *somewhere* in South America.

Or thereabouts . . .

At twenty to five there was a muffled explosion in the simmering hold. It seared Deckie Sullivan's face like a parboiled lobster, scattered smoking embers over a wide radius across the after decks, and stopped every man dead in his tracks with the new fear erasing every trace of relief generated by our landfall.

Because that violent warning told each and every one of us that, instead of hours, we could now be several days from outside help. That we had finally run out of time.

The offshore wind, you see, had steadily risen to a now blustering force six and *that* – unless we found shelter soon – would draw the already awakened fire into a raging inferno which we couldn't hope to overcome. But a hastily approached lee shore, in the part of South America that I thought we were closing, wouldn't necessarily offer any of the other luxuries we'd so fervently looked forward to.

Like being able to risk leaving the bloody ship, for instance.

Unless, of course, we elected to die in a rather novel manner for deep sea sailormen.

Of snake-bite, say. Or disease or poisoning, or simply good old-fashioned malnutrition. Hopelessly lost in the biggest, most horrifying jungle hell in the world.

Part II

6

So now we really did find ourselves trapped between the Devil and the deep blue sea. In the most literal and nerve-prickling sense imaginable.

Ahead of us lay that big-ship seaman's most dreaded nightmare – a totally unfamiliar and uncharted land mass – stretching from horizon to horizon across our track with, perhaps, submerged shoals and reefs reaching towards us this very minute, waiting to tear the bottom out of the *Maya Star* as we searched for a sheltered anchorage.

That, then, was my Devil – and most certainly one I didn't know.

Yet my original intention was now out, at least temporarily. By which I'd hoped to close the coast until we could make out detailed features. Should the immediate landfall offer little prospect of habitation – such as buildings which might house doctors and radio sets, and condensation-sparkling bottles of chilled beer – then I'd proposed to alter to port or starboard on the carefully considered spin of a coin, running parallel to the land until we found what we so urgently needed.

But that wishful thought was *before* number five had exploded back into life. So now my only alternative would be to turn and run with the freshening wind, hoping that our speed under full revolutions might neutralize the drawing effect of our passage on the reviving blaze. Yet even then it could still take ten, maybe twelve hours of fire-fighting to regain control – *if* we ever succeeded at all ... and running at eighteen knots would take us damned nearly two hundred miles back out again. Right to where we'd bloody well started from.

With the added hazard of having to spend a whole night lit up like a homing lantern for every Tom, Dick and Hermann to pinpoint as a potential target.

Either way, however, that provided my only deep blue sea option. And I'd been there before.

I wondered what it was going to be like. Shaking hands with the Devil ... ?

From that decisive moment we only did one of two things. Led by Chippie most of the deck gang returned wearily to a very familiar battle with the fire, working all the time with muscles knotted into wire strands, simply waiting for that five hundred ton time bomb in six to touch off right alongside them – while the rest of us applied ourselves to driving a deeply laden ship on the end of a crackling field telephone, into a haven which we didn't even know existed ... across shallowing, completely unknown waters ... in a hurry. And in rapidly falling darkness.

Which meant our muscles were just as tensed as the fire brigade's. The only difference was that, while we waited apprehensively to go straight down, Chippie's crowd were rather more preoccupied with the prospect of going straight up.

Apart from seaman Sproat, that was. He simply crouched there and watched through those dull, brooding eyes of his. And, just occasionally, allowed the brief spark of madness to vent from that splinter-damaged brain.

Eventually, however, Ainslie gripped the binoculars hopefully and called in a tight voice, 'There! An opening ... Just to the right of those low cliffs.'

I grabbed for the proffered glasses and refocused with nervous fingers. The darkness was closing in fast now, yet

98

we were still a good five miles offshore. Unless I could establish an approach heading very shortly we would *have* to turn away and head back out to sea. I knew I could never get the *Maya Star* close enough in across that steadily shallowing water to obtain any shelter from the wind which was now drawing long, curling tongues of flame clear out of five and over the coaming to the base of the mainmast.

But cliffs maybe fifty, sixty feet high *did* hold a promise of a lee anchorage. And when land meets sea at a vertical angle it should also indicate a deep water entry – if there wasn't a sand bar or an off-lying rock shelf blocking the seaward channel.

And *if* I wasn't doing all the wrong things anyway. Just steaming on a hope and a prayer . . .

I handed the telephone link from the bridge to the after steering position over to the Third Mate. Cleese was on the wheel but his view forward was non-existent, every swing of the ship's head would require to be monitored from the vantage point of the ruined bridge and I mentally congratulated myself that at least I'd had the foresight to organize direct lines both to the poop and to Second Engineer Nolan down below.

'We'll go in,' I said, trying to hide the doubt in my voice. 'Bring her over to starboard first, Three Oh, until you have the entrance in transit with that mountain peak inland. Con her down it but f'r Chrissake don't let us blow off the line.'

Lifting the glasses again I strained to pierce the gloom ahead. Within the next few minutes we'd only be left with the featureless silhouette of the land to guide us, which was why I'd to select our leading marks quickly . . . that black, distant peak would always be visible against the night sky while I hoped we would retain sight of the lighter foreground patch indicating Ainslie's cliffs, constantly nearing as we were.

Though if we did lose them, or touched bottom as we approached anyway and lay aground without that essential shelter from the wind . . . well, the *Maya Star* would burn uncontrollably to the waterline before tomorrow came. Until she blew up, that was. While my mistake would have killed all of us, beginning with the seriously wounded and finally taking the last soul among us. I knew that much already with chilling certainty, because I'd already made out enough detail of the land we were so rashly closing – and all I'd been able to make out was a wild, impenetrable torment of jungle foliage as far as the eye could see.

Picking up the engine room phone I spun the handle. It was answered immediately from below. Nolan sounded tired and it was almost possible to sense the pain in his distant tone, even distorted as it was by the background clamour of the engines.

'We're nearly there,' I shouted. 'Go on stand-by from now on in . . . and, Archie.'

'Yeah?'

'We could touch, an' God knows what the bottom's like. If she starts to make water below jus' get the hell out, don't wait for an order. Just stop engines and come up.'

He said calmly, 'Aye . . . Aye, we'll do that.'

I lifted my eyes to the patch of cliff. We'd soon know what the bottom was like, and if it lay less than twenty-eight feet from the surface Second Engineer Nolan and Greaser Hotchkiss would probably be the first to find out.

'Dead slow ahead both,' I ended, feeling the revs dropping away before I'd even replaced the hand-set. I walked to the after end of the bridge and looked over. Dramatized by the half light the scene around the fire-stricken hold made me wonder, with rueful cynicism, whether I ever really had awakened from my nightmare of last night. Or was I still that lost captain piloting an eternally damned Flying Dutchman, with black troglodyte sailor-souls labouring incessantly around a reflecting, swirling inferno . . . ?

'Evenin', Mister B!'

I started. Bosun Fletcher stood below me with the reel of the hand lead in his arms. He turned and followed my eyes aft for a moment, then swung back and grinned savagely. 'At least the young un c'n brew us another cuppa tea . . . I'll away down to the chains an' get ready. You'll be wantin' a few soundings as you go in, eh?'

'Bose,' I called with heartfelt sincerity, 'I plan to feel our way in like a blind man on a tightrope.'

Fletcher started down the ladder. 'Don't feel bad about it. Even he'd 'ave ter take a few chances – if 'e'd got a red 'ot poker up *his* ass!'

I heard him again, a few minutes later, with the visibility now clamped down so the shoreline merely displayed itself as a darker border to the glint of the sea. Then the Bosun's clear tone floated up from where he hung out against the restraint of the projecting platform.

'Byyyyy the mark . . . FIFteen!'

Fathoms, that was. And the ship already less than a mile from that lighter patch of rock still discernible ahead. Ainslie muttered hopefully, 'Plenty of water up to now, anyway.'

I didn't answer, just leaning over the remains of the bridge wing and feeling the hot, putrid breath of the off-shore wind tugging fretfully at my shirt sleeves, swamping me with the sick-sweet stench of rotting vegetation.

'An' a haaaalf . . . FOURTEEN.'

Shoaling steadily. Just what we'd hoped for.

'And a quarter . . . FOURteen . . .'

We could keep her going until Fletcher found five fathoms. After that the *Maya Star* would need wheels . . . 'Starboard five,' the Third Mate passed down the telephone link. '. . . *Mid*ships!'

Our raised foc'slehead swung slightly and steadied on the rock face ahead, a faint blur now, bisected by the vertical line of the shot-away foremast. Above us the funnel purred raspingly, spewing a trail of diesel exhaust which eddied and tumbled aft along the boat deck. Between that and the noxious gasses pouring from five hold, both Cleese on the wheel and Sparks on the telephone must be sucking for breath, even through the wetted masks they'd tied over their faces . . .

'Byyyyy the deep . . . TEN.'

Shallowing much faster now, and still a good half mile to the faint indication of the only haven we were likely to find on that nerve-racking approach. I literally ground my brows into the soft rubber cups of the Barr and Strouds, hungrily trying to pick some detail from the irregular silhouette of the land.

Until . . .

'There *is* an entrance,' I snapped suddenly. 'It has to be either a river mouth or a creek. Those cliffs seem to follow inland on the port side, then . . . then water – maybe a half mile width of water . . . and the opposite bank. Probably jungle there, right down to the shoreline . . .'

'An' a quaaaaarter . . . NINE.'

'That went down quick,' the Third Mate commented uneasily.

I muttered 'Mmmmmm,' and kept on staring through the glasses. There wasn't a lot to add. Unless it was a prayer. The biggest danger lay in the overall length of the *Maya Star* – nearly five hundred feet. Which meant that by the time Fletcher, situated in the chains below the bridge wing, had retrieved his lead line, felt in the darkness for the tell-tale strips of leather or bunting or linen which would indicate his current sounding, and called them to us – then the actual ship's forefoot, already two hundred feet ahead of the Bosun, had probably travelled twice that distance into completely unknown and now rapidly shoaling water.

Which meant that we could be running hard aground under our bows while there was still enough water to cover the *Maya Star*'s decks amidships. While if there happened to be a vertical rock *shelf* lying in wait just ahead of us . . . with the juggernauting kinetic energy generated by even a slowly moving vessel weighing several thousand tons . . .

'BY the deeeeeep . . . EIGHT.'

Fletcher's unhurried roar. Too dark even to pick out the white splash of his lead as it swung forward to curve gracefully down and beneath the surface. But the water was calmer here, finally we were beginning to feel the benefit offered by the shelter of the land. No splashing little whitecaps now, only the oily scend of the swell encroaching on the shore.

Suddenly I froze, staring hard through the glasses out to starboard – a creamy swirl was breaking in a long line just off our bow . . . a sand spit. Stretching an almost imperceptible finger out to sea and roughly parallel to our heading. I chewed my lip thoughtfully. Oddly enough the tension had left me now, allowing my mind to concentrate with cold detachment on the task in hand, and that spit looked good, lying as it did. It suggested we'd made precisely the right approach to line up with the deeper channel that *must* be cut by the flow of the anonymous river ahead.

Unless it veered sharply. Or it wasn't a river at all, and I was simply steering fifteen men and a simmering time bomb up a non-existent creek without a bloody chance to turn and come out again . . .

'Nothing to starb'd, Three Oh,' I cautioned.

'Annnd a quarter . . . SIX,' the Bosun bawled.

'*Christ!*' I added. And grabbed for the engine room phone.

The Second's voice came back right away. Very tightly.

'Stop engines . . . Slow astern both.'

'Slow astern, Sir . . . Both engines goin' astern . . .'

The deck stilled temporarily and then began to bounce rhythmically beneath my feet. 'Watch her head doesn't swing off, Ainslie,' I snapped, feeling the tension flooding back in an apprehensive surge. Had I pushed our luck too far, should I have approached even more cautiously and the hell with what that fetid wind was doing to our presently secondary hazard . . . ?

'By the deeeeep . . . SIX.'

Still carrying way but only more slowly now, with the black water slipping along our flank in a gentle ripple. I leaned over and peered aft, even masked by the glow of the fire I could make out the white water creaming in under the *Maya Star*'s counter as the astern power dragged us to a halt.

'Cleese reports losing steerage way, Sir.'

Whizz the phone again . . . 'Stop engines!' Rush back to the bridge wing and stare penetratingly at that rock face, so close now that even through the darkness I could make out little clumps of trees and plants clinging to the crevices . . . but they seemed to be coming even nearer. We were swinging to port, in towards that bloody great slab of South America . . .

'Slow ahead *both*, Archie . . . ! Starboard twenty the wheel.'

'An' a haaaaalf . . . FIVE.'

'*Jesus!* And if we've only a few feet under us amidships, what the hell's left under the bow?'

Then I spun frantically again with everything seemingly crowding in on my over-taut mind at once. The anchor party . . . Had Chippie gone forward to stand-by at the windlass like we'd previously arranged, or was I conning a half-ship in the middle of the night, in the middle of a converging nightmare, without even a hook to hang on to if the unknown quantity of the current caught our head and swung us inexorably into the side?

'And a haaaaalf . . . FIVE.'

'CHIPPIE . . .' Me bellowing from the bridge with the panic surely apparent to every ear aboard ship. But Ainslie cool as a winter wind.

'Steadying now, Sir. Cleese has her again.'

'CHIPPIEEEEEEE!'

'Aye *aye*, Sir . . .' from the foc'slehead. A bit plaintively, as if wondering what all the fuss was about. I hung weakly over the rail for a moment feeling the relief dulled by a blinding rage with myself, partly at having forgotten to check he was there and partly because I'd had so little faith in the old seaman that I'd felt the need to.

'Stand-by to let go,' I called unsteadily from between cupped hands.

The ship moving steadily ahead. Well past the cliff at last with a long thread of silvery water leading maybe half a mile into the narrowing channel. But narrowing how quickly? I suddenly lifted my head – the wind had gone completely and from where I stood I could see the flames from number five were only rising vertically now, without the same curling anger as before. The blaze already seemed smaller, too, with the smoke lessening and the steam increasing.

'By the deep . . . SIX.'

Easy, Barton boy, don't push your luck any further. Not tonight, not in this bloody cloying darkness . . .

'Stop both, Archie,' I said into the phone and then, when the way had finally come off the *Maya Star*, I leaned out over the bridge front for the last time that day and roared 'LEGGO FORR'AD . . . !'

The anchor went immediately, rampaging riverwards in a deafening clatter of snaking, rumbling chain, entering the still water with a monstrous splash, and with the rising cloud of dust from the cable locker forming a billowing fuzz against the deep purple sky.

I felt the fatigue sweeping over me in great floating waves but I didn't stay on the bridge. I following Ainslie down aft, towards the haggard, stumbling men who still drove themselves to fight a fire. I wasn't aware of any sense of triumph because I knew we hadn't really won a victory. Oh, maybe we'd won a skirmish, gained a very brief respite, but that was all. Because we still couldn't afford to risk leaving the ship to venture over to that threatening, anonymous shore – certainly not until daylight and probably not even then, judging by what little I'd already seen of the impenetrable nowhere I'd brought us into.

So we were still as much at hazard as we'd ever been. And

still many miles and many hours from civilization and outside help even when, and *if*, we finally quenched the fire in the *Maya Star*.

We'd simply varied the nature of the threat, that was all. Exchanged the familiar menace of that deep blue sea for the completely alien embrace of the jungle.

Like fish. Out of water. And the frying pan already heating on the stove . . .

But we did win the battle in the end. Still not the victory, but at least a little part of our own very personal war.

And by the time the sun touched that Red Duster, flying doggedly from the *Maya Star*'s poop for the second morning since her agony had begun, there was no more fear of her exploding without warning. Or only a very small fear perhaps, because the serried rows of lyddite-charged shells in number six were still hot and still menacing, but they would gradually become cooler now as the remaining heat in the extinguished number five hold dissipated.

There was no fire left. Only a buckled, twisted shambles that had been the after well deck, with a tangle of filthy hoses and wires and cables interweaving with the ruptured crates of cargo and, over everything, that solidifying spew of yellow-ochre slush which seemed to add a deliberately mocking splash of sickly colour to the desolation. Our war wasn't a grey war any longer. It was a yellow war now, the colour of putrefaction. With the black soot veins of cancer lacing and oozing and spreading remorselessly throughout.

And then we slept. Even when the sun did begin to lift the clinging mist which drifted across the oily water and reveal the first hints of the green tangled mass that formed our temporary haven, there was no man aboard who did more than cast an apathetic, red-rimmed glance outboard before sinking gratefully into the slime where he'd stood for so long.

We'd won our preliminary battle, yes. But only at the expense of a crew now reduced to a ghastly resemblance of those walking dead creatures of my nightmare. It was another irony – that the wounded were now the strong, and Thomson with that blown-away stump to his shoulder, and Second Engineer Nolan all shiny with the suppuration of festering burns, and a Lamptrimmer without a scalp and very little left of an ear – that they should watch over the ship while we, the lucky survivors, succumbed to the exhaustion of success.

Seaman Sproat didn't watch over us, though. Seaman Sproat wasn't able to watch over anything because he was mad with a steel splinter in his brain and a simmering, homicidal promise of coming horrors in his unblinking stare.

In fact Seaman Sproat frightened me more than any hot cargo of explosives.

But I still slept like a corpse. Even with the two of them aboard I slept until three-o-clock that afternoon. I didn't dream at all that time.

It was only when I awakened that the next nightmare began.

Strangely it all started with a rather ordinary cardboard box. The Third Mate was already watching it idly as I walked up the foc's'lehead to join him after I'd first surfaced from the near coma of exhaustion.

He'd obviously had the same thought as myself – to check on the *Maya Star*'s cables and make sure they hadn't fouled as she'd swung with the tide. We'd moored to a second anchor during the night, fires and physical tolerance notwithstanding because, as soon as we'd had an opportunity really to assess the width of the deep water channel, I'd decided we had to restrict the radius of arc through which our stern would swing when the ebb gave way to the flood tide – and quite justifiably as it happened. The sounding Fletcher took over our counter as we first lay athwart the river at four in the morning showed our propellers only just clearing the bottom.

'At least we don't have to worry 'cause we're blocking the

entrance,' Ainslie reflected cynically. 'It's sure as eggs are eggs no other vessel's going to want to come up *this* particular creek to the back've beyond.'

I concurred gloomily. The light of day had only confirmed my earlier impressions of a totally undeveloped and uninhabited Amazonian rain forest. If any sort of people existed in this particular part of the world then they had to be as primitive as a stone-age axe. I had an unsettling memory of boyhood yarns which all seemed to revolve around great white hunters battling against hordes of pigmies who sprayed curare-tipped darts with devilish accuracy . . . or had that been in Africa? At least I was pretty certain my navigation hadn't been *that* unreliable, so we weren't likely to find ourselves up against a battalion of six and a half foot tall Zulus . . . or was it South America which had the Zulus . . . ? But that was the trouble with being a sailor – the average seaman's geographical knowledge quite often only encompasses a half mile radius of his ports of call . . .

A splash and a sudden swirl from the shoreline opposite made us both glance over anxiously. A semi-submerged shape cut a slow vee across the surface and I swallowed uneasily. 'Crocodile?' I ventured . . . or were they alligators around here?

'I don't think I want a run ashore, thank you,' the Third Mate said very positively. 'Anyway, where d'you reckon we really are, Sir?'

I shrugged. That was the problem I'd been applying myself to since last night, but in all seriousness I did have a pretty good idea.

'Somewhere in the Amazon Basin, probably south of the main estuary . . . I think there's another maze of inlets and tributaries in what's called the Rio Para. That puts us maybe fifty to a hundred miles from any kind of civilization.'

'What do you plan to do now, then?'

I watched the crocodile thoughtfully. There were an uncomfortably large number of its friends lying like rotting logs in the mud along the water's edge. 'Get the hell out've here,' I retorted. 'Just as soon as we can weigh anchor.'

Voices from behind made us turn as the Bosun and Chippie climbed the ladder to the foc'slehead. Arguing volubly as usual.

'. . . big as . . . as a rolled-up 'atch tarpaulin', I tells you,' the Carpenter swore heatedly. Fletcher gazed at his adversary with monstrous contempt. 'Lyin' git, that's wot you is, Carpenter . . . go on then – if it wus *that* big you jus' tell me 'ow you got out've its jaws an' we'll *all* 'ave a bloody good laugh!'

'Jabbed me screwdriver innits eye, din't I?' Chippie offered with saintly virtuosity. 'An' when it opened its mouth ter yell I ups an' offs like a gale o' wind f'r safety, see?'

'Ohhhh I *see*, don't you worry,' the Bosun jeered heavily. 'I *see*, all right, Carpenter . . . an' what I see is a lyin', dodderin' old drunk what can't tell the diff'rence between a crocodile an' a bottle've rot-gut rum, thass what *I* see . . .'

'Don't you call *me* a drunk, you drunk!' the Carpenter shrieked. 'Right then . . . ! *Right* then, Bosun bloody Fletcher . . . I'll *show* yer the screwdriver. The very screwdriver I'm tellin' yer about, an' it still with blood an' bits've eye stuck on it . . .'

'We'll be going on stand-by for sailing in about twenty minutes,' I broke in impatiently. 'Once I've had a last look round the ship and seen Gifford about the wounded.'

'Twenty minnits? Aye, Aye, Sir,' the Bosun growled. 'An' if that old idjit's goin' ter try an' work the windlass up 'ere, I'd be obliged if you could let me take the wheel on the poop, Mister Barton. At the other end've the bloody ship from '*im*.'

'Oh God,' I brooded irritably. 'Who needs a whole world war with those two around . . . ?'

'That box,' Ainslie murmured pensively. 'It might be worth having a look at. Assuming it's come in with the last tide it could maybe give us some indication of where it was jettisoned. A local harbour maybe, or settlement.'

I leaned over the bulwarks and looked down. The box lay close by the swirl on the surface marking the point of entry of our starboard anchor cable, held by a trailing wire binding snagged through one of the huge links. Even from my height of eye there did seem to be some legend stamped on it and I stepped back, nodding.

'You may as well try and recover it. Get someone to shin down the cable – *with* a safety line, mind – and grab it. One thing, it can't have been in the water very long. It's floating too high, no time for the cardboard to become saturated.'

I turned away and forgot about the flotsam box.

For a little while.

Gifford met me at the doorway to the saloon, now turned into our makeshift hospital. His face was even more morose than usual despite the few hours sleep he'd been forced to take.

'Thomson's bad,' he said. 'That arm's beginning to inflame an' there's stuff comin' out of the stitches. I reckon it's infected.'

I passed the back of my hand across my sweating forehead. There was nothing we could do – apart from sail as soon as possible and find a doctor. Somewhere. Or even a mission station where they'd have proper antiseptics, though I didn't know whether we weren't too late for that already.

'Let's have a look,' I muttered apprehensively.

Which we did. While I felt myself going pale despite trying desperately to look cool and unaffected. 'What can you do, Gifford? It could take us hours of coast hopping before we sight a hopeful prospect – possibly not until tomorrow. Maybe there's a blackout in force along this coast even. Then we're unlikely to pick anything out until daylight at the earliest.'

The Second Cook chewed his lip absently, eyeing the scarlet stump with professional detachment. 'I could put a tube in it, maybe. As a sort of drain for the poison.'

Thomson hadn't moved, not even when Gifford had gently removed the dressing. He simply lay there with eyes closed and only the faint rise and fall of his perspiration-shiny chest to show he was still alive. I said quietly, 'Thomson . . . did you hear that?'

He opened his eyes and blinked up at me. Swallowing nervously I forced a smile. 'Chef wants to mess you about again. Can you stand it, son?'

'He's doin' his best is the Second Cook, Sir. Whatever he says . . .'

He closed his eyes again for a moment, then re-opened them so suddenly I felt a slight shock. 'Sir?'

'Mmmmmmm?'

'This morning . . . while you were all sleeping, and Lamps an' me was watchin' from the deck. I . . . I *felt* something, Sir. Something not right.'

I frowned, glancing at Gifford queryingly from the corner of my eye. 'Your arm, you mean . . . Being painful?'

He shook his head tiredly. Uncertainly. 'No, Sir. It was something to do with the ship . . . about the jungle out there. As if we were, well, as if we were bein' *watched*, Sir. From the trees. By something . . . or someone.'

And I can't really explain why, but I swear the hairs on the back of my neck began to prickle at the way he said it. But I just smiled that forced smile again and shrugged.

'Crocodiles, probably. Or monkeys or some other creatures. There're some pretty curious local residents wondering what the hell we're doing up here, remember?'

He sank back and seemed to drift off to sleep almost right away, and that in itself worried me. But so did the expression on the wounded steward's pallid features. As if he knew how wrong I was, but that we'd soon find that out for ourselves . . .

And all the time I was having a look at the Lamp-trimmer's fortunately uncomplicated head wound, and at Seaman Sproat's so terribly complicated incipient madness, I was uncomfortably aware of one thing.

That Thomson could just conceivably be right. And that there *was* some alien presence hidden in that green, decomposing nightmare out there.

Just watching us. And waiting.

Not that it mattered, of course. Seeing we wouldn't be remaining in that unsettling, claustrophobic anchorage for more than another few minutes.

I'd done what necessity had dictated and supped with the Devil for as long as convenient. Now it was more than time to slip out of that temporary haven of his and head back to the deep blue sea. Then, once out, bring the *Maya Star* hard round until we were heading a mile off and parallel to the shore, full ahead both for safety and peace.

And the big sigh of relief I'd faithfully promised myself as the last of our ammunition cargo was transferred to some other poor bloody first mate's ship.

I stood up there on the bridge and glanced critically astern. Fletcher was already standing-by on the wheel with Cleese now taking the telephone beside him. The deck throbbed excitedly with the renewed rumble of the slowly-turning engines, making the whole ship feel alive and almost . . . well . . . cheerful, somehow. As if the prospect of heading seawards was already acting as a salve to her earlier wounds.

Face forward, and Chippie standing at the windlass controls waiting for word to commence weighing. The huge warping drums revolved adding yet a greater sense of urgency to the event . . . Only Ainslie was still missing, still engaged in recovering that intriguing cardboard box of his. He'd shinned down the cable himself in the end, with a safety line bent around his waist and an accompanying barrage of cheerful advice from the grandstanding crew, like: 'Don't you worry about them crocs, Sir. They only likes the fat uns like Ricketts there . . .'

Or, rather more wistfully from the Bosun, 'Let the

Carpenter go. 'E'll not *need* a safety line . . . jus' 'is bloody *screw*driver.'

I watched as the dripping carton was hoisted over the flare of the bulwark first, followed by the Third Mate, and felt a little surprised when he seemed to ignore the repartee all of a sudden, just grabbing the box from Ricketts and hurrying aft towards the ladder.

Still, we'd had a hard time, all of us, and shinning down anchor cables takes a lot of effort even when you're normal . . . I looked anxiously at my watch. Soon the tide would turn again and the *Maya Star* would begin to swing as the force of the ebb took over, turning her through a hundred and eighty degrees to face back up river and away from that silvery, beckoning seascape. And that would mean a further delay because I couldn't risk trying to turn us short round in the width we had to spare, so it would be daylight tomorrow before we dared to move from here. I began to wish irritably that I hadn't let Ainslie bother recovering that bloody silly box.

And then he arrived on the bridge anyway, and I snapped shortly, 'Come on then, Mister. Everyone's waiting for you to . . .'

But then I simply ground to an uncertain halt, staring blankly at the battered cardboard case he held out towards me.

'Not been in the water long,' the Third Mate snarled almost accusingly. 'You said it yourself, Sir – it couldn't've been jettisoned all *that* long ago . . .'

But I hardly heard him. I was too busy trying to understand the threat which I knew *had* to be presented in the black-printed legend across the otherwise inoffensive scrap of flotsam.

And finally I did understand. Only too well. Slowly I picked up the engine room telephone and spun the handle. Nolan's distant voice sounded cheerful. 'Ready to go when you are, Captain.'

I opened my mouth, then shut it. Then opened it again,

still looking at the box. 'Finished with engines,' I said with almost masochistic deliberation. 'You can shut them down again, right now.'

There was a moment of silence, then he said, 'Would you care to repeat that?'

'I say again – shut down the bloody engines, Mister Nolan. And come up on deck.'

I dropped the phone back into its cradle just as Ainslie let the carton fall to the scarred planking. The printing on it looked much too innocuous, really, to make a man change his mind about sailing a ship to sea. I didn't even understand what the legend said, for that matter.

Apart from . . . *Gänseleberpastete*.

In German.

7

'My foreign languages are almost non-existent,' Ainslie muttered a few minutes later. 'It's some kind of goose product, I think. Liver paté, maybe, and tinned . . . you can see the rings of bases impressed on the bottom.'

'From an officers' wardroom, no doubt,' I completed savagely. 'Aboard a certain *Kreigsmarine* commerce raider I happen to know of.'

I smashed my fists hard on the rail and stared angrily out to sea, but even that had suddenly changed now. It didn't look inviting any longer, or friendly. Only dangerous again, like it always did when the bloody war reached a bit too far and touched you.

'You think it's the same one we met before?' the Third Mate asked. I shrugged. 'Probably. Too much of a coincidence for two of them to be hunting the same area.'

It was his turn to kick the bridge front in angry frustration. 'Two hundred, two-fifty miles we've steamed since then. And a dog-leg course at that. Yet we're *still* within gun-shot range of the bastards!'

I'd have preferred a less succinct choice of phrase but I only chewed my bottom lip in brooding concentration. 'The point is – how long can a cardboard box float before it softens and disintegrates. Five hours . . . ten?'

'Say ten. It's as good a guess as any.'

I frowned. There was something niggling at the back of my mind, something I couldn't quite pin-point, but the logic of the argument did seem inescapable. 'All right, ten hours. So assuming a rate of drift of one knot shorewards that would put the position of its original ditching as being within ten miles of the coast.'

'Yes, but on the same presumption that *was* ten hours ago,

115

Sir. She could be another hundred-plus miles away if she'd held a straight course, even at cruising revs.'

'*If* she did. But she's a spider, remember? She doesn't really need to go looking for victims . . . people like us are always passing by so all she needs to do is wait. And watch.'

'Meaning she could still be out there. Maybe just over the horizon?'

I shrugged tiredly. 'I think I would be if I was that raider's captain. Why burn my own limited fuel reserves when other people are falling over themselves to run into a stationary trap . . . and this is far enough away from the positions where we and that other British merchantman were attacked in. The one which left the machine-gunned boat.'

He seemed to slump visibly. As though all his optimism had finally been used up. 'Then what *do* we do? Stay here for ever, f'r Chrissake . . . Or just till the bloody war's over?'

I didn't trust myself to answer right away but he must have seen the anger in my expression because he said quickly, 'Sorry, Sir. But I can't help thinking of the wounded. Thomson especially. And Sproat.'

I dropped my eyes to the foc'slehead. Chippie had already screwed the windlass down again and now the crowd were desultorily trailing aft in a disconsolate, silent group.

'I've got to think about all of you,' I said quietly. 'And the ship. If saving the ship wasn't important, and the cargo she carries, then we wouldn't have been running down this coast in the first place. And next time we meet Jerrie we won't get a second chance, Mister Ainslie. No way will they let us go a second time.'

The youngster blinked at me through red-rimmed eyes. 'Then you intend to stay here, and the hell with the wounded?'

I swung on him. 'I intend to stay here and keep the wounded *out* of hell if I can, Ainslie. How long d'you think Thomson could stay afloat beside an abandoned ship without an arm? And Sproat – who hasn't got the mental ability to bloody well walk now, never mind swim? And the Second Engineer . . . what the hell d'you imagine immersing those burns of his in salt water would do to him? Even if they don't machine-gun us all anyway, before we've even time to *hit* the bloody water . . .'

I halted abruptly with the rage inside me dying away to a shamed silence. The Third Mate was still staring at me but now I could see the tears trickling slowly down his cheeks, and I suddenly realized he was crying. Just like a frightened little boy.

Or a man. Who'd watched too many shipmates die already, and who still couldn't see an end to it all.

I turned away towards the ladder with the sadness and the sympathy reflected in my own eyes. But perhaps I'd known all along that opting for the Devil, and consequently spurning the deep blue sea which had been a part of me since boyhood, wasn't a thing a man could ever do without, at the same time, handing the initiative over to the Devil.

In fact I should have appreciated the risks a long time ago. After all, I had been warned, hadn't I?

The ship had tried to do that much herself. And now I'd trapped her as well.

It was too late to do anything more to safeguard the *Maya Star* before darkness fell that night. There was something about this jungle river, something I knew Thomson had already felt and which made other eyes turn uneasily outboard to scan the bright green wall flanking us. Something which told me not to take any risks.

So I called the crew together on the boat deck. I considered it necessary for morale, simply that they should understand the reasoning behind our additional period of detention, virtually marooned in the Amazon delta . . . perhaps only by my imagined fears, but isolated neverthe-less as surely as any ship on a solid reef.

'Forty-eight hours.' I said, watching the assembled faces for the first signs of dissent. And there was a certain resentment at first, but there was discipline there too and that overcame the natural tendency of most seamen to complain bitterly and with enormous logic about every conceivable thing – and then get on with doing the bloody job anyway.

'We stay for forty-eight hours and then we sail. And we don't put in again until we're sure there are the facilities we need.'

'Yessir,' the Bosun grunted, adding the force of his own majestic eye to my own scrutiny. 'Forty-eight hours. Right, Ricketts?'

The A.B. looked blank as ever. Just nodded vaguely. 'Aye aye, Bose. Like you says.'

'Carpenter?' Fletcher probed maliciously. Chippie started to go red in the face the moment his adversary's eye fell on him.

'Don't you try an' tell *me*, Bosun. I does what the Cap'n sez an' I don't need no common bloody *sailor* ter . . .'

'Gifford?' the Bosun continued with a pleased, snide grin on his florid features. But even a bit've gratuitous aggravation was better than no warfare at all.

But the Second Cook was made of sterner stuff. 'Why forty-eight hours? Why not four days, or eight or ten?'

'Because we can only assume that the raider won't risk remaining in the same place for too long, Gifford. While he may not have to hunt for passing targets at first he soon will, certainly after a few sinkings. A diversionary route will be established round the immediate area and he's out of business till he opens shop somewhere else – apart from the fact that the Navy are following every lead on *his* whereabouts at the same time.'

'An' what about my blokes. The wounded?'

'I'm sorry. They'll have to take their chance.'

'Well, I don't like it,' Gifford muttered aggressively. 'I don't like it one bit an' that's tellin' you straight, Captain.'

I eyed him warily. Gifford could mean trouble if he wasn't brought up with a sharp round turn. 'I didn't ask you to like it, Second Cook. But by God you'll *do* it . . . or turn over tending the wounded and spend the rest of the voyage in the bloody forepeak! Do you read me loud and clear, Gifford?'

But even then it was a delicate balance. The truculent chef glowered resentfully across the deck towards me and I couldn't help feeling uneasily that it only needed one little push to send the rest of them into a state of near mutiny.

Until Chippie sidled over to Gifford and, very matily, whispered something into the tough little cook's ear before winking and moving away again. I frowned but, as Gifford didn't seem to be doing any more protesting, carried on.

'At first light tomorrow we prepare to move the ship further up river if there's enough water to float her. I want her hidden by the bend from any prying eyes from seawards . . . Bosun.'

'Aye, Sir.'

'Have the motor lifeboat ready to slip by dawn. Mister Ainslie will stay aboard here while you and I sound the channel to chart a passage . . .'

. . . and so we began to plan our next two days. Yet all the time we were doing so I could feel that niggling doubt at the back of my mind, the one which seemed to cast a shadow over every decision I'd taken since we'd first found that enigmatic piece of flotsam from what could only be an enemy warship lying somewhere out there.

Couldn't it . . . ?

There was one other minor riddle which had intrigued me. I managed to corner Chippie on his own after I'd broken up the briefing.

'What the hell did you *say* to Gifford. To make him so amenable?'

The old carpenter grinned a very mischievous grin. 'I jus' told 'im how I could see his point o' view, an' that I wus very pleased 'e had such consid'ration f'r others. In fact, I even offered ter show my appreciation if 'e wanted to argue the toss a bit further wi' you, Mister B.'

'Appreciation . . . How?'

'By pattin' 'im on the head, Sir. With me fuckin' mallet!'

I spent a long time that evening in simply walking round the ship, really understanding for the first time how badly she had been damaged, and just how lucky we'd actually been even to have made it this far.

It was getting dark by the time I finally left the saloon and by then I did feel a little happier. Thomson's arm didn't seem any worse while the tube Gifford had inserted into the festering wound appeared to have eased the pain, probably through relieving some of the gathering pressure.

The Second Cook had looked a bit more settled too, since his friendly chat with the Carpenter, and I wondered absently if there weren't more ways than one of skinning a cat. Under the circumstances I'd always tried a soft approach until now, yet this evening when I'd first stuck my head somewhat challengingly around the door of the make-shift hospital and snapped an uncompromising 'Captain's rounds, Gifford. Get on your feet and report!', he'd simply broken off his conversation with the Lamptrimmer, swung smartly and answered, 'Yessir! Nothin' to report except the steward's improvin' a bit. Sir.'

Even Seaman Sproat hadn't got any worse. But then again, Seaman Sproat hadn't got any better either . . .

Gifford had hesitated as I stepped out on deck again, and called gruffly, 'Earlier on, Captain. I guess I wus wrong – about sailing right away an' that.'

But I didn't do more than fix him with a bleak stare. 'Just check your blackout's secure, Gifford. And stick to your own job while you're signed on articles aboard this ship.'

He looked back at me without any malice at all. 'With respec', Sir, but if I'd done *that* all the time . . .' he said dead-pan, 'I wouldn't've been sewin' the steward up like I did . . . I'd've roasted 'im. Wi' potatoes an' gravy.'

We both began to grin at the same time. But I didn't think I'd have any more trouble from Second Cook Gifford.

Not as long as I kicked him occasionally.

Bombardier Timmer was cleaning the gun when I arrived on the poop, with enormous enthusiasm and a great deal of hot, soapy water. The Third Mate was there too, along with young Sparks and Able Seaman Cleese, polishing and greasing both the working parts and each other with equal fervour while Apprentice Meehan collected empty ammo cases which had lain since the first, and last, time we'd used the bloody thing in action.

All the same, I didn't say too much. I knew we were never going to need it again but the sight of Ainslie's face – preoccupied with this rather irrelevant attempt to get back to some kind of normal routine as opposed to his earlier strain on the bridge – even that was enough to quash my initial bitter reaction, now curiously akin to old Jeremy Prethero's aversion for the sinister, inadequate weapon we mounted.

'Planning on croc shooting tomorrow, Bombardier?' I kidded with weak jollity. Until his eyes, serious as ever behind the huge spectacles, unexpectedly lit up with a disturbing, battle-orientated hope and I was uncomfortably reminded of a previous occasion when our earnest military presence had shown an equally animated reaction to the prospect of continuing a gunnery duel . . . and that time he'd been prepared for round two with a whole warship, not just a reptile.

'*Could* we, Sir . . . ? Just a few rounds, test she's still O.K.?'

'God almighty, no!' I protested hurriedly. 'We're supposed to be in hiding – not give a Brock's Benefit for every Indian within twenty miles. Beside which, we don't even know if the natives are friendly.'

'Pigmies,' Sparks offered knowledgeably. 'You get pigmies around the Amazon, so I believe.'

'Ah,' I said. 'I was wondering about that. I knew they were either very big or very small.'

'It doesn't matter,' Bombardier Timmer hinted darkly. 'Not when you point a 4.5-inch gun at them . . . if you were sure it would *fire*, anyway.'

'*No!*' I emphasized stiffly. 'Clean it if you want to, Timmer. But keep your hands off the trigger.'

I think he was going to say more, the way his eyes glinted with disappointment behind the spectacles, but then he stepped back into the bucket – which seemed to be standard routine for Timmer during gun cleaning – and the ensuing gust of laughter rather killed any further protest he'd intended. Seeing him do that gave me another uncomfortable twinge, though, and I made a firm resolution to keep Bombardier Timmer well away from the ammunition in number six from now on. If he'd been as accident-prone when he was handling *that* a little earlier we'd have been staging a spontaneous Brock's Benefit for half the South Atlantic ocean . . . while that thought left me unhappily conscious, once again, of the fact that we were still living aboard a highly unstable floating bomb, and right in the middle of nowhere in particular.

'I was thinking, Sir,' the Third Mate asked diffidently. 'We've still got two boats . . . If I took, say, the motor lifeboat close inshore and up the coast there's a chance I could find somewhere reasonably close to here. I could even pick up a doctor . . . ?'

'Forget it, Mister Ainslie. The fuel won't carry you far, while you might have a two hundred mile run and still find nothing. That's partly the trouble, we don't know a damned thing about this area other than that distances in the Amazon Basin are virtually beyond comprehension . . .'

'Four thousand and fifty miles, Sir. That's the actual length of the Amazon itself, supposed to be.'

We all turned and looked at Apprentice Meehan in surprise. He fiddled with the empty shell case he held and looked embarrassed. 'Go on, son,' I encouraged. 'What else can you tell us about it?'

'Oh . . . er . . . well, its navigable length goes as far as a place called Iquitos, Sir. About two and a half thousand miles up river, but there's also a maze of tributaries entering the main course – the Purus, the Madeira, the . . . ah . . . Japura an' Morona an' the Xingu . . .'

I blinked at the youngster with respect. The new generation of sailors after the war would be very different. If enough of them lived to see it. 'Now d'you understand what I mean, Three Oh? We may as well be on the moon for all the help we can expect from the outside world.'

'Even the mouth of the Amazon's over fifty miles wide, Mister Ainslie.'

'And it would be a helluva time to find *that* out,' Sparks added. 'If you got half way across and a force ten blew up.'

I looked at him sharply, but I didn't know why. Just something in that innocent remark that made me uneasy again . . . I shrugged it off.

'Better get some sleep, anyone who's not on anchor watch. We're off at five in the morning, remember. Into the white man's grave, eh?'

I wished I hadn't said that. As soon as I saw the expressions on the faces around me I wished I hadn't said a bloody silly thing like that.

There was still a sluggish mist hanging over the river when we were ready with the motor boat moored and waiting at the foot of the pilot ladder. It would be another half-hour before the heat of the sun cleared away the last traces of a tropical jungle night, but already the trees themselves were alive with the weird animal sounds of unseen creatures surrounding the *Muya Star*. The crocodiles were awake too, or at least as awake as their reptilian sluggishness would allow. I had a rather unsettling conviction though that, if one of us accidentally slipped over the side, those distant logs would become remarkably mobile. And very suddenly indeed.

However our task was in the middle of the channel – if a channel there was – and a reassuringly safe distance from the shallower water which seemed to mark crocodile territory. I hoped, by means of the lead line, to chart a deep-water track to take us further up river, at least to a more sheltered mooring position round that bend some half a mile ahead. If there was a *Kreigsmarine* surface raider lurking somewhere out on that sparkling sea then I didn't want the *Maya Star* standing out from the green jungle like a target at a fairground.

It was a bit ironic, really. They'd gone to a great deal of trouble to paint us grey all over because we were at war . . . and they'd still been wrong. They should've made it a nice dappled brown and green instead. Like a bloody tank.

There was an almost festive air about the boat's crew as we headed away, an excitement more suited to a party of picnicking school children than a boatload of war-weary merchant seamen. Even Bosun Fletcher had apparently got over his latest brush with the Carpenter earlier this morning when he'd sardonically asked Chippie to lend him his screwdriver . . . 'Jus' so's I'll have a bit o' *protecshun* from them crocklediles, heh, heh.'

To which lure the Carpenter had refused to rise, merely counter-attacking with a crushingly off-hand, 'Jus' stick yer head innits eye, Bosun. It's gotter sharper point than anythin' in *my* tool chest.'

Myself, Fletcher on the lead, Hotchkiss tending the engine with a constant stream of encouragement, Ricketts and Cleese and Sparks simply sitting for most of the time and thoroughly enjoying the adventure . . . we really did begin to feel we were off on a good, old-fashioned pre-war jolly the next two hours as we laboriously charted a passage towards that bend in the river.

Quite early in the proceedings, Cleese had taken the tiller to allow me to concentrate on plotting the soundings as Fletcher stood up in the bows, casting the lead well forward of the stem with an easy underarm action then, as it came up to the vertical, dunking it critically before calling the depth.

'By the maaaaark . . . seven.'

The sweat ran down my arm and smeared across the back of the chart I was using to make notes. Even though I was probably enjoying the break as much as any of them I still wished I could have turned the chart over and used *that* side to navigate the *Maya Star* into harbour. It was one of the few rescued from our single unburned folio and it said *Thames estuary – southern part* . . .

'An' a quarter . . . SIX, Sir.'

The boat butted contemptuously through a small eddie and a fan of spray hissed inboard, curling back over the gunn'les to spatter along with my sweat over the chart. I wiped it away, leaving a muddy brown streak across the sheet.

'Wind's gettin' up again,' Hotchkiss remarked to no one in particular.

I glanced up towards the approaching bend. More than enough water so far anyway but I'd been kept busy noting leading marks to guide us along the deepwater track. There was certainly a channel but it wasn't very wide, and even with the present survey I knew my nerves would be kept pretty stretched, conning the *Maya Star* around that curve.

'A quarter less seven an' still mud bottom . . .'

'You wouldn't hardly know she'd been on fire,' Sparks murmured absently. 'Not from this distance.'

Swivelling on the thwart I followed his gaze astern to where the ship lay. From here, maybe half a mile, she really did look good too, apart from the dark stain along her boat deck and the sadly misshapen lines of the forward centre-castle where the wheelhouse had once glinted so proudly in warm varnished teak, she seemed as neat and clean as ever. Though admittedly the funnel *was* a little crooked, and the amputated foremasthead did give her a slightly down-in-the-mouth aspect . . . through a seaman's eye, anyway.

'An' a haaaaalf . . . SIX,' the Bosun called.

So far so good. Those two big trees in transit now and us almost on the bend itself . . . just about here I'd have to start giving the ship ten of starboard wheel to ease her on to the new heading . . .

'Permission to come port a bit, Sir,' Cleese asked. 'There's a clump of floating stuff up ahead an' I don't know what's under it.'

'Cut it close as possible,' I said. 'This is the critical section we're in now.'

Hotchkiss just had to crane his head forward and pass a comment as usual. 'Jus' brushwood, Sir,' he offered helpfully. 'Jus' blowin' along the surface like an East Indiaman under full sail . . .'

I glanced up irritably, fighting off the temptation to tell Hotchkiss to stick to running the engine and leave the navigation to the seaman branch. But I never did . . . I just took one casual look at the spindly, dead mass of thornwood scudding across the sluggish water, noticing the way the wind carried it relentlessly seawards even though the flood tide was still running fairly strongly . . .

. . . and then I froze. For one long, disbelieving moment I simply froze with my mouth open and my eyes gazing hypnotically at that pirouetting, breeze-driven puff-ball of jungle vegetation.

As with sudden, startling clarity I finally understood what had been nagging so intermittently at the back of my mind all this time. The one factor which hadn't fitted in with our theories about the origin of that ominous scrap of galley refuse entangled in the *Maya Star*'s anchor cable . . .

Until finally I found my voice with a conscious effort. 'Bring her about, Cleese. *Quickly* now!'

The seaman blinked at me disconcertedly but it didn't really register – my abrupt change of manner.

'Bring her *about* . . .' I snarled again, with the fear in me honed by a blinding self-recrimination. 'Hard a PORT, man, an' head for the ship for *God's* sake!'

But still Cleese sat transfixed, hand gripping the tiller and a look of utter astonishment on his face. Or more of nervousness, really. Like the expressions a soon-to-be-dead captain and a shortly-to-be-legless Quartermaster Tennison had shown a million years ago, when I'd stormed into that wheelhouse after a certain yellow-funnelled stranger had first revealed her true intentions.

In fact they were *all* gazing at me now, the whole damned lot of them in that boat. Desperately I dragged Cleese bodily from the sternsheets and threw the tiller hard over as Sparks stammered an unsteady, 'Sir? What the hell d'you thi . . . ?'

'That box!' I spat, the guilt burning more and more fiercely as I really appreciated what a stupid, elementary miscalculation my tired brain had committed. 'That bloody *box*, Mister Martin! The one we all assumed had been carried ashore with the tide . . . Well it *couldn't* have been, dammit! Not when all the recent weather's been from inland an' liable to catch a high-floating carton the same as it's doing to that brushwood over there, pushing it clear over any flooding tide like a yacht running before the wind . . .'

Fletcher frowned enormously, uncomprehendingly. 'You tryin' to say it didn't, then . . . come from a Jerrie?'

We were virtually travelling sideways now, the boat listing crazily under full rudder but still continuing to open the last few yards of the bend, skidding and overshooting the last fronds of concealment offered by that green jungle bank.

'I'm saying it didn't come from any German warship out at *sea*, man. I'm saying that bloody box just had to have been ditched UP river from where the *Star*'s lying . . .'

But then we'd cleared the corner altogether. And there really wasn't any need for me to complete my so-brilliant but so-late deduction. Only I did anyway, because of all the bitterness and disgust I felt for myself.

'LOOK!' I snarled uncaringly. 'There's the origin of that cardboard carton, Fletcher. Only she's been here all the time, dammit . . . She was anchored here before we even *arrived*!'

8

In actual fact she didn't look at all warlike at first sight, that ship at anchor maybe four cables up river from us. Even I blinked uncertainly, beginning to wonder if my logic hadn't been too logical, my fears too automatic after the strain of the past few days.

I didn't settle the boat back on course, though. I just held that tiller hard over and kept turning away, praying to God they wouldn't see us during our brief personal appearance . . . and at the same time stared grimly at the alien vessel, tightly assessing the lines of her with a seaman's eye and a pessimist's apprehension.

She didn't have a yellow funnel now, for a start. And while there *was* still a deck cargo it looked different, canvas-covered and irregular instead of the clean white-wood packing cases shipped by our earlier attacker. But there was the same rakish style to the superstructure, while the flared bows had a character and an individual grace which were unmistakable.

I knew I hadn't been wrong. Not within the last sixty seconds anyway . . .

'It's her,' I snapped. 'The same bloody raider.'

Yet they'd been clever, the men aboard the ship ahead. They'd subtly altered details here and there, not many but enough to lull any challenging naval vessel into making a doubtful, time-wasting check. If a general description *had* been transmitted by any of her victims, then the new-look livery of that innocent freighter would certainly take time to verify – and time was all they needed. Just a few minutes grace to close within range of, say, a British cruiser's guns and then . . .

'Bastidsl' the Bosun ground. But there was an almost

comical resentment in his voice behind the natural fear, and I followed his eyes to the stern of that sea-wolf-in-sheep's-clothing until I saw precisely what he meant.

'Bastids!' Fletcher snarled again. 'The cheeky bastids!'

Because they'd added one more touch which was guaranteed to make any R.N. unit think twice before opening fire. She wasn't flying Spanish colours any longer. She wasn't flying *any* kind of neutral colours now, come to that. In fact for sheer, swashbuckling *panache* I just had to take my grudging cap off to a certain *Kreigsmarine* commander.

You see, it did look so damned convincing, fluttering brightly over the raider's counter. That Red Ensign – of our own British merchant fleet.

But then everything seemed to start happening all at once and I knew with a sinking heart that the Devil hadn't finished with us yet. Not by a long, nerve-rending way.

The raider first . . . Men running forward, up the sheer of the foc'slehead to lean over and point. Other men, all dressed in ordinary merchant seamen's rig scurrying down the accommodation ladder towards the ship's boat moored alongside . . . Two sailors dragging the canvas cover off something secured to the starboard bridge wing . . . why did they need a *bearing* compass f'r Chrissakes . . . ?

'It's a machine-gun,' Fletcher corrected abruptly. 'They gotter machine-gun on the bridge . . .'

'Open her *UP*, Hotchkiss!' I yelled, with the fear now in full command. 'Get that bloody engine goin' like you never ran an engine before, man.'

Shouts as well, drifting across the space between us, vaguely intelligible even above the frenetic putter of our engine . . . '*Raus, raus!*' An' there's no way c'n they pretend *that*'s a British seaman's call to all hands . . .

Almost back in the cover of the jungle now, though, with the after end of the warship already hidden behind the bend. My mind rapidly seizing in a blundering mesh of uncertainty – What to do first . . . ? Could we hope to get the

Maya Star under way in a frantic attempt to clear this confined river before they overwhelmed us? Should we just slip both cables and let her go – or would the raider still catch up with us out at sea and . . . ?

But then I didn't even have time to worry about the immediate future. Because I was too stunned by the crazily escalating events of the moment, when . . .

'Down river Sir!' Cleese shouted suddenly, unsteadily. 'Between us an' the *Star* . . . there's a boat. An' it's comin' to cut us off.'

I remember I started to say idiotically, 'Don't be so bloody silly, Cleese . . .' because we'd got enough trouble already and how in hell could a boat be on *that* side of us when nothing could possibly have passed us without being seen on our way up river . . . ?

. . . But then I ground to a speechless halt, and simply stared at the impossible motor launch ploughing from the vegetation-concealing bank on a steadily closing interception course with ourselves.

For that was the precise moment when I suddenly remembered what the wounded Steward Thomson had whispered last night – first suggesting that other undefinable unease which had stayed with me ever since. When he'd said so positively, '. . . as if we were, well, as if we were being *watched*, Sir. From the trees. By something . . . or someone.'

And now – far too late once again – I was beginning to understand.

That the *Maya Star had* been watched from the very first moment she entered this death trap. That any naval officer worth his salt would have immediately established an observation post seawards, and that all the time we'd been hiding there, being about as inconspicuous as a skyscraper in a desert, the enemy we'd been at such pains to conceal ourselves *from* had simply been watching, and waiting . . . but that conclusion in itself opened yet another line of

130

imponderables. Such as, why? Why not just go for us right away? Steam a few cables until their line of fire opened up and then blast . . .

'*Achtung!*'

'They're hailin' us,' Hotchkiss muttered, unnecessarily as ever seeing there wasn't one man aboard who wasn't eyeing the other boat hypnotically anyway.

Apart from me. I was too busy scanning the river bank on either side for a landing place – anywhere I could run the motor boat aground and allow us to take to the jungle. Only we'd really be in the hands of the Devil then, half a mile from the *Maya Star* in what looked like virtually impenetrable undergrowth. And crocodiles . . . crocodiles all along the bank, watching us. And waiting. Just like the bloody Germans . . .

'*Achtung, achtung!*' Both the command and the threat were unmistakable this time.

'I'll acktung the bastids,' Fletcher breathed ominously, feeling at the same time for the engine starting handle in the bilge. I trapped it with my foot and snapped, 'Belay that! They've got guns f'r Christ's sake.'

'They won't need them,' Sparks commented bitterly. 'They've cut us off from the ship already.'

I hoped he was right – about the guns. But I couldn't get the memory of that bullet-riddled and empty lifeboat we'd found out of my head. Along with all the other nightmares that crowded in on it.

'Cut the engine,' I called heavily.

Hotchkiss stared at me disbelievingly, it was the first time I'd ever seen the little greaser at a loss for words. I didn't waste time explaining the facts of war to him – there wasn't time for that, not judging by the way the four ratings now visible in the launch brought their submarine-guns to the ready, while the fifth man, wearing a white service cap, cupped his hands from the sternsheets and roared uncompromisingly, '*ACHTUNG*! You will heave-to immediately or my men will fire . . . *Verstehen, Kapitän?*'

'Cut that bloody *ENGINE*, Hotchkiss,' I shouted furiously.

'*Do* it, ye stupid idjit,' Cleese literally screeched with the tension of it all. 'Jus' *do* it afore they cut us ter bloody pieces . . .'

But even then things wouldn't stop piling in on us during that crazy, outrageous venture into the back of beyond. I just remember slumping on the thwart with the galling hope that I would merely be a prisoner of war in the next few minutes and not a bullet-torn corpse floating monstrously down river towards the place where the crocodiles smiled . . .

. . . when a very strange incident occurred. Quite suddenly, and without any warning.

As a great column of mud-brown water climbed shockingly from the surface between ourselves and the converging enemy.

While the reverberating detonation of that inexplicable event sent a thousand wheeling, screeching jungle birds high into the blue equatorial sky.

I do remember thinking one more thought with a great deal of gloomy satisfaction – that the Hun with the white cap in the other boat was looking every bit as shattered as I was.

Maybe he wasn't as scared as me, I'd got a pretty good head start on the terror trail, but by God there was no Teutonic pre-planning about whatever was happening now. Somebody had engineered a very explosive surprise for each and every one of us aboard those wallowing craft.

Dimly I was aware of the bows rising to the blister of water displaced by the impact and automatically steered her into it, while the spray from the subsiding column hazed across us in a vicious arcing tattoo.

And then we heard the next one coming. 'Geddown!' Fletcher spluttered. 'Get yer 'eads DOWN, lads . . .'

Which was a pretty irrelevant thing to suggest under the circumstances, but at least proved I wasn't the only non-thinker in the Amazon Basin that moment . . .

Just as the incoming roller-coaster stopped dead.
BaROOOoooom!

More filthy water . . . spray . . . a great rolling surge of brown liquid shying us over on our beam ends . . .

'Oh Mary Mother've God look down on us an' gie us yer . . .'

'ShuRR*UP*, 'Otchkiss!'

'. . . s'well as the Father an' the Holy Ghost . . .'

'That was a shell,' Sparks stammered uncomprehendingly. 'Someone's firing *shells* at us f'r . . .'

I lifted my head above the gunn'le . . . Oh yeah, not only had the Bosun told us to get our heads down, but I'd gone and done just that. And blinked dazedly around for some clue, any clue, to tell me what the hell was happening.

And then I saw it. A third flash and a gout of smoke from seaward – all in the same split second as I registered that the German launch had abruptly sheered away now, running desperately for the cover of the far bank. And then the shell landed . . . further away from us this time . . . and almost beside that other refuge-seeking craft.

'It's our own gun,' I bawled above the slamming explosion. 'They're firing from the *Maya Star*. Timmer . . . an' that damned contraption of his.'

'Shall I still cut the engine then?' Hotchkiss blurted apprehensively. I swung on him with shameless hypocrisy.

'You do an' I'll have your guts, laddie! Jus' keep her going like the clappers . . .'

Slam! From the battered but apparently unbowed ship at the mouth of our ridiculous, ill-chosen refuge.

BOOOOOOOOM! Yet another detonation with the noxious mud fountaining and the spray falling back towards the surface in a hanging, shimmering cloud . . .

'GETTEM!' Fletcher was roaring now in a positive hysteria of revenge. 'Gettem an' blow them bastids' guts all over the blurry jungle . . . Feed 'em ter the crocklediles, me hearties . . .'

And Cleese jumping up and down with the relief of it. 'Oh

you lovely boys . . . Oh you *loverly* boys, so help me y'are . . .'

Slam!

I began to feel sick. Maybe it was inconsistent of me after my earlier terror, but I was only conscious of a wave of sympathy for those five targets in that fleeing enemy craft. I'd already been there, simply waiting for my name to be engraved on the next one to home in, and I knew the blood-freezing chill of it.

And then the inevitable happened.

'God, but they've been hit!' Sparks said in a funny, doubtful voice and I glanced at him in surprise, it seemed an odd way to report a victory. But then I saw the expression on his face too, and realized I wasn't the only one with mixed reactions to salvation. Even a very temporary salvation like the one we were currently offered.

'We hittem!' Fletcher and Cleese and Hotchkiss and Ricketts were all yelling in a frenzy of joyful togetherness, until I watched as the spray from the last round cleared and then snapped sharply, 'Belay that! Stand-by to pick them up, all of you.'

Because by then I could see that the explosion had been beside, rather than in the German launch and now she lay with only her port gunn'le above the surface and a ring of threshing black dots already breaking the lyddite-tainted swirl.

'Ah, leave 'em,' the Bosun growled, while there was a resentful look in his eye which saddened me and showed just what the euphoria of war can do to a man during the killing time itself.

I slammed the helm hard over, staring at him bleakly. 'I said we pick them up, Fletcher. You do just that.'

'I done somethin' else a few days ago, Mister Barton. I helped you bury a lot o' our shipmates because've them, remember?'

And I did remember. While I also hadn't forgotten that they'd abruptly left us aboard a burning ship and a long

134

way from anywhere. But I still intended to save as many of those floundering enemy sailors as I could – even at the expense of revealing that my motives were a little less than purely compassionate.

'That raider can blow us to hell in two minutes flat,' I retorted coldly. 'Maybe, just maybe, they won't be quite so keen to act in haste if we're holding some of their own crew aboard the *Star*. As hostages.'

For a moment longer he glared at me then, ever so slowly, his expression cleared as he began to grin a thoroughly unashamed grin.

'You're as big a bastard as me, Cap'n,' he said with enormous respect. 'You're jus' quicker to catch on. That's all.'

I didn't say anything. I knew he was wrong somewhere but it didn't really matter and I needed to concentrate on bringing us alongside the capsized boat . . . I threw a quick, apprehensive glance astern, feeling the muscles tight in my back with the anticipation of a second launch taking up the chase. But there was nothing to be seen in the direction of the bend. Even the bows of the raider were out of sight now, almost as if she didn't exist.

'Ready to cut her back,' I called to Hotchkiss.

One of the men in the water began to scream, '*Hilfe! Mein Augen . . . Kamerad, bitte . . .*'

'They're not so tough,' Fletcher observed with deep satisfaction.

'I think he's been blinded, dammit!' Sparks flared.

'Stop her, Hotchkiss . . . and get a move on in the bows. We don't have much time.'

We began to drag the shocked, weakly-struggling German sailors inboard. As I kept an uneasy watch over that uncomfortably silent river I also stole an occasional glance seaward, to where my own ship lay at anchor.

There were figures clearly grouped around the gun on her poop and I couldn't help reflecting what ideal targets they presented for a single sniper hidden in the flanking jungle

. . . and despite our present unexpected reprieve began to feel more and more despondent, more and more helpless in the face of what appeared to promise inevitable defeat.

Because the *Kreigsmarine* didn't even need a whole warship to batter us into flaming submission.

Just one man, with a rifle. And the *Maya Star* would be without any defence at all.

Ainslie and Chippie were waiting as I swung my leg over the bulwarks.

'Get a cargo net rigged. We've got wounded men in the boat.'

'Ours?'

'Theirs . . . And it's the same raider.'

The Third Mate nodded calmly. 'We guessed that much. Did we do right this time . . . opening fire?'

I smiled humourlessly. 'Tell Timmer I'll buy him a beer sometime. He's a very good gunlayer.'

Ainslie smiled back. It was funny but now we were really up against it he seemed a lot more settled, almost resigned. Like the now-dead Quartermaster Tennison had been the first time we met our enemy. I could only hope that Ainslie wouldn't finish up the same way.

'He drinks Newcastle Brown,' the youngster said. I turned to stare back up the still unnervingly deserted river and frowned ruefully.

'He may have to settle for a Pilsner – brewed in Munich!'

The rest of the survey crew clambered inboard and turned to haul the cargo net containing the first German sailor over the rail. It was the man who'd been blinded by Timmer's last shell. We couldn't help staring curiously, a little nervously, but he looked remarkably young and not at all superhuman. A flap of flesh hung over his eyes where a splinter had caught him and it didn't look very good to me.

'Get Gifford,' I muttered. 'Not that he can do all that much.'

The rest of our prisoners were manhandled gently on

deck. They were all pretty badly shocked and at least two were moaning softly with badly smashed limbs. The last man was different, though. He wasn't wearing his white uniform cap any longer but the voice was the same as the one which had first called on us to '*Achtung!*'

He used it again despite the gaping wound in his thigh. '*Heil Hitler!*' he spat from the deck, and the way he threw it at us made me go cold. But not the Carpenter.

'Who's he?' he asked, looking all mystified.

The Bosun shrugged. 'I dunno. One've the Jerrie officers, I s'pose.'

'Not him,' Chippie retorted. 'I mean that Hile Hitler 'e's on about?'

While the expression of hate in the German's eyes proved he could understand, as well as give orders in English.

'Get them up to the saloon,' I snapped hurriedly. 'And have two men guarding them all the time . . .' I swung back to face the stern, but there was still no signs of movement from the hidden warship while I was becoming more and more apprehensive. For the first time I was beginning to appreciate myself what Tennison had meant – about being more scared by the anticipation than by the actual event.

'Nolan's already on stand-by down below,' the Third Mate volunteered tentatively. 'And there's power to the windlass . . .'

'Forget it,' I heard myself say. He looked at me a little surprised.

'We could be weighed and out to sea in half an hour, Sir.'

I shrugged, not taking my eyes off that curve in the river. 'So could they. And I've a very strong feeling that's just what they want us to do – get the hell out've it.'

Ainslie turned and followed my gaze. I could also see Timmer and the other men grouped around the gun doing precisely the same thing. I couldn't help noticing that one of them wore a white bandage around his head and recognized the old Lamptrimmer, back in fighting trim again. It made me feel a bit proud, seeing that, and I knew I couldn't afford to make any more mistakes. They'd endured too well so far for me to let them down again.

'Why . . . ?' the Third Mate muttered petulantly. 'Why the devil *are* they waiting?'

I glanced at my watch. It was nearly midday.

'We'll wait as well,' I said. 'We do nothing either. Not for a couple of hours, anyway.'

But I thought I was beginning to understand. Only hazily, but at last I did think I knew why.

I desperately hoped I was right, and that I could find some way of solving an apparently insoluble stalemate. Because if I couldn't, then I was about to throw away probably our most precious asset.

I was handing over to the Devil our last chance of escape.

We waited a long time before they finally came.

I think we remembered the heat most of all. From a blazing oppressive tropical sun beating over the almost deserted decks of the *Maya Star* while at the same time the putrid, insect-plagued miasma of the jungle enveloped us in its claustrophobic embrace.

None of us said very much. We didn't have to. The unspoken fears were revealed in our nervous glances outboard, and in the way fingers constantly played with clothes or rails or scraps of cod-line, and every head would start anxiously at the shocking screech of tree-borne monkeys or the snapping of a twig under the passage of some invisible creature. Or more especially at the sullen ripple caused by a water-breaching saurian.

And so we simply waited. With the engines slowly turning over and the soft splash of the outboard discharges as the only indication that the ship really was still alive and not already a part of that secret, twilight-filled place. While sometimes, even above the sounds of the jungle, a moan or a whimper would carry down from the saloon which served as a pathetic substitute for a hospital. Only now even the curses of pain were alien, cried in a gutteral foreign tongue, and yet we still blanched a little because they undoubtedly meant the same thing whatever the language . . . that war and hatred were synonymous with suffering.

We waited . . .

We waited, and watched the bend in the river with an almost hypnotic fascination, ensuring that enigmatic twist in the watercourse was always covered by at least one pair of unblinking eyes and the black muzzle of a very old gun. While close by the gun were men, always Bombardier Timmer among them, simply standing in desultory groups or sitting in tight-lipped readiness for something, anything, to happen.

And that was the period during which I began to realize that a change had come over the *Maya Star*'s complement, because while the unease at what that 'something' might be was still present, there was a new determination evident as well, a sort of bloody-minded self-satisfaction in the fact that we *were* staying to see it through this time; that we'd finished with running and hiding and that even though our war was still more than one-sided at least we did intend to fight one, not keep turning the other cheek for slap after slap.

And then the 'something' finally did happen. But even then the manner of it was so unexpected that it left me even more confused, more uncertain that I could ever be a match for the Devil . . .

'Thomson's gettin' worse again,' Gifford had whispered quietly in the corner of the sweltering saloon.

I looked at the Second Chef and even as I did so I was aware of other eyes watching me from behind. Or two pairs of eyes to be more specific – the pained but still bright-with-hate glare from the young Nazi captive, and the more brooding, burning stare from mad Seaman Sproat. And now it was difficult to say which pair of eyes made me feel more uneasy, and more frightened.

'How bad?' I asked. Gifford didn't hesitate, he just shrugged and avoided my stare.

'I think he's dyin', Mister Barton. An' there's not a bloody thing I c'n do, not even to make it easier for 'im.'

I didn't answer. There wasn't a word I could say which was going to add one more minute to the steward's life-span . . . and I admit I actually felt shamefully relieved when Apprentice Meehan tumbled into the saloon at that moment, his face a conflicting mixture of excitement and sheer trepidation.

'A *boat*, Sir . . . coming down the river towards us!'

I swung, snapped, 'Watch those prisoners!' at Hotchkiss and Ricketts – standing guard with grimly uncompromising expressions reinforced by large teak-wood battens – and began to run. Even so, by the time I'd reached the poop the approaching launch was maybe a hundred yards away and still closing steadily.

Ainslie met me at the head of the ladder. 'They're flying a white flag, Sir. I think they want to talk.'

Pushing through the group of men around the gun I saw that Timmer was already in the gunlayer's seat, hands caressing the laying handles with just enough control to keep the muzzle deflecting steadily, constantly trained on the enemy craft. But I also realized that within another few minutes the barrel would have reached maximum depression, the raider's emissary then being shielded by the sweep of the *Maya Star*'s counter . . . Scrambling aft I leaned out over the taffrail, cupping my hands.

'*ACHTUNG! Nicht* . . . Oh hell, Ainslie! What's the German f'r keep off?'

He screwed his face up, then said helplessly, 'I dunno.'

'Try firin' the gun at 'em,' Fletcher growled dangerously. 'That'd give 'em the messidge.'

I yelled, 'Heave-to where you are. *Nicht* come closer . . . *verstehen*? *Halt machen sogleich* or else . . .'

A sharp command carried across the water and immediately the boat lost way and lay just stemming the tide. This time there were six sailors seated stiffly across the thwarts, all in tropical uniform now and smart as a lick of new paint, but I was more preoccupied with the officer standing in the sternsheets. He looked as cool and as formal as if making an inter-ship visit during a Spithead Revue. There was a slightly mocking tone in his voice as he called back to me.

'I suggest we talk in English, *Herr Kapitän*. Do I have your permission to come aboard?'

I hesitated. From above there were certainly no weapons to be seen in the boat and it *was* a pretty laborious way to hold a conversation. It didn't seem to be in what I imagined must form the strict conventions of parley either, yelling at each other across a fifty yard gap, so I jerked my head at Fletcher.

'Drop the pilot ladder to the water . . .' I turned back to the rail. 'Have your boat put you on the ladder then stand off again. But only yourself, Mister. None of your heavy mob, understand?'

'I'll take a steel block wi' me,' the Bosun promised darkly. 'Any nonsense an' it'll be through their bottomboards quick as a Bishop's kiss . . .'

I didn't discourage him this time.

Though it still didn't seem to be a match for half a dozen five-inch guns and a few torpedo tubes. Or even a sub-machine-gun.

I arrived on the forward deck as the German swung his leg over the rail. For a moment we inspected each other warily and I couldn't help reflecting ruefully that his side appeared rather more than in control of this particular bit of the war at the moment – he being immaculate in freshly laundered white ducks while I must have appeared as some survivor from a holocaust.

Which I was, on consideration.

He saluted formally while I inclined my head in return. I

noticed he gave the old-fashioned naval acknowledgement though, and not a Nazi straight arm. He didn't suggest we hailed Hitler either, like our earlier unwilling visitor had done.

'*Kapitänleutnant* Flindt, navigating officer of the German Naval commerce raider *Seepanther*. You are the captain of this ship, Sir?'

I shrugged. 'The captain is dead. I am in command.'

'I'm sorry.'

I looked at him. 'Are you?'

He nodded, but there was a remoteness there which indicated platitude rather than gut-feeling. 'The war can be a hard taskmaster, *Kapitän*. And you were most irresponsible in returning our fire.'

'Captain Prethero was dead long before we did,' I snapped. 'And you've admitted that we returned your fire, Mister. That means you also agree you opened the action first.'

He didn't even blink. 'You used your radio in direct contravention of the Geneva Agreement . . .'

'Forget it,' I ground wearily. 'You can tell 'em how we attacked you with a radio later. At the war crimes tribunal, after we've won the bloody war.'

Just for a moment his glance took in the gutted and forlorn superstructure, and the tilted funnel with a hole in it, and I could see the sardonic flicker of disbelief at such an unlikely event ever taking place. But then he turned back to face me with that impeccably correct expression of detachment.

'My captain has sent me in the hope that further violence will be unneccessary.'

I was still angry but I couldn't help a twisted grin. 'Agreed. You tell him that if he surrenders by four-o-clock we won't shoot at him again, Lieutenant.'

But I didn't generate any reaction even then. Sure as hell of himself he merely smiled deprecatingly and gave a funny little bow. '*Touché, Herr Kapitän* . . . ! Now perhaps we can be serious, please?'

'But I *was* being serious,' I retorted.

The smile still remained but now there was a slight stiffness to it.

'I am instructed to inform you that my captain is prepared to allow you to take your crew by ship's boat to the nearest safe refuge. Your vessel will remain here as a lawful prize of the *Seepanther* . . . You have my assurance as a German officer that you will leave unharmed, and that any stores or medical supplies you require will be provided on request.'

I took a deep breath. A very deep breath.

'I've got a much better idea,' I retorted as calmly as I could. 'Mine is that we sail this ship out of here altogether, using charts provided by you . . . and what's more, that you remain for at least six hours longer. Until we're well away and hull-down over that horizon out there.'

He blinked, just before his mouth screwed into an uncertain grimace which held more than a touch of outrage. 'This thing you are proposing – it is *Geistesgestörtheit* . . . madness, Sir! To imagine my captain would allow it.'

I shrugged. 'O.K. Then suggest to your captain that he takes up, say, big game hunting to pass the time. The next few months are going to be very tedious. For all of us.'

Over the German's shoulder I could see Ainslie and Fletcher eyeing each other blankly, but it was nothing compared to the expression on *Kapitänleutnant* Flindt's aquiline features.

'I am sorry, but I do not understand, *Kapitän*. Explain yourself.'

'Oh, but I think you do, Flindt. In fact I think it's the only reason you're here right now, talking, and not sitting behind those bloody guns of yours happily shooting the hell out've this ship . . . because you daren't, dare you, Mister? Lift one finger against us as long as we sit here.'

He didn't answer. While the outrage had now given way to naked discomfort. I took the opportunity to underline what we both knew, though. Just for the pleasure it gave me.

'Because the *Maya Star* is blocking your only exit channel out of here, isn't it, Lieutenant . . . ? And if you sink this ship your own precious *Seepanther*'ll be trapped in this jungle backwater until hell itself freezes over . . .

'. . . so how's that, Mister – for stalemate.'

Though actually my own feeling of self-satisfaction at the German officer's discomfiture was wearing a bit thin before I'd even finished speaking. Because the trouble with stalemates is that nobody can be said to have won.

. . . I wondered irrelevantly if they'd lend *me* a gun. To pass the rest of the bloody war on alongside their captain!

You see, there was one flaw in my strategy . . . that even if the enemy agreed to allow my outrageous demand, there was still absolutely nothing to stop them breaking their word and following us immediately the *Maya Star* was clear of the narrow channel.

And I had a sudden chilling recollection of a machine-gunned lifeboat which suggested that war, in the *Seepanther*'s case, was a very serious business. Unless I could use my other trump card . . .

'Well?' I snapped with a matter-of-factness I certainly didn't feel. Flindt swallowed and turned to me with the composure firmly back in place.

'It may be possible. I will have to receive fresh instructions from my captain.'

'You get them then! And there's another small matter for his urgent consideration – our guarantee of safe conduct.'

The German frowned. 'Guarantee?'

'We have five of your men aboard, Mister. And I intend to keep them here as an insurance policy, at least until we're well away from the range of your guns . . . *verstehen?*'

I could see it had come as no surprise to him, which had presumably been another reason for the velvet glove approach. But he still stared at me tightly, resentfully. 'That will not be permitted, *Kapitän*. You will return those men before any further negotiations are carried out. Any agreement will be adhered to most conscientiously by ourselves regarding your release.'

I shook my head emphatically. 'Like the Geneva Convention, f'rinstance? Which you just happened to overlook when you opened fire as soon as we transmitted . . .'

'That is your interpretation only.'

'An' it's *my* ship that's blocking the fairway . . .' I shook my head again. It was my turn to look sardonic. 'I don't plan to make the same mistake twice in one voyage, Mister. You may also remember the last time we met . . . you must've known you'd hit us hard yet you still broke off the action and left us to fry aboard a blazing runaway two hundred miles from anywhere – and if *that* wasn't in breach of the rules for humane warfare then I don't know what is, dammit!'

'*Nein!*'

I blinked at him in surprise, the denial was so emphatic. But he continued in a less aggressive tone.

'Your gunner was fortunate in hitting our steering compartment during the preliminary stage of the engagement. We were forced to withdraw immediately . . . that is why we are in this place, *Kapitän*. We have been making urgent repairs.'

'*Forced* to withdraw, Mister? When you've got twin screws and are still manoeuvrable enough to make this lousy entrance . . . ? Yet you claim you were *forced* to withdraw, and so quickly you didn't even have time for the accepted practice of ensuring our boats were adequate for survival?'

He shrugged. 'Would you have remained if you had been our captain? Please remember that your gunner was continuing to return our fire, and that we are a lone wolf with limited repair facilities . . . a further hit putting even one of our engines out of action and we would have been crippled, with no hope of evading your own Royal Navy which is combing the area in search of us.'

I hesitated. If Flindt was telling the truth – and it did

seem at least a plausible reason for their apparent callousness – then our own super-zealous Bombardier Timmer had virtually prevented medical aid from being made available from the *Seepanther* itself. Yet even that wasn't any cause for resentment against our earnest soldier, because the corollary to that was that Timmer had also saved the *Maya Star* from being sunk in the first place . . . as well as her surviving officers – myself, Ainslie and Second Engineer Nolan – from the normal fate of being taken for eventual transhipment to Germany as prisoners of war.

But that thought, in itself, raised my other question . . .

'All right,' I probed cleverly. 'Then explain the boat we passed on our way here, riddled with bullets. What happened to the poor bastards aboard that ship, then?'

And I was so intent in pressing my own argument that, while I noticed the flicker of sudden inspiration in his eyes, it didn't really register at first. Not that I'd virtually handed him one of my own trump cards on a plate.

Until he said calmly, 'That was an already damaged lifeboat from a British ship called the *Wellington Court*. She crossed our path *en route* and was abandoned before we sank her with gunfire. All her crew are safe and will, I trust, make a landfall on this coast within the next few days.'

'The boat?' I pressed doggedly. 'Why the bullet holes if you're so tremendously humane, Flindt?'

He shrugged again, watching me with an almost amused eye. 'I have told you – it was not required by the *Wellington Court*'s crew. We machine-gunned it in order to sink it. We do not like to leave unnecessary evidence pointing to our whereabouts, you understand?'

But I was still being clever. Far too clever for him.

'Ah,' I said. Cleverly! 'Then you can presumably show me those officers of hers which you undoubtedly hold aboard the . . . ah . . . *Seepanther*? Because I'm not a trusting man *Herr Kapitänleutnant*, so I won't believe your next statement – when you tell me you didn't take prisoners on that particular occasion. Out of sheer humanitarian considerations, of course.'

The only snag was that he didn't look at all uncomfortable now. Or trapped by my superlative logic.

Because he just smiled a very open smile, and said, 'But I have no intentions of denying the fact, Sir. You see we do hold the *Wellington Court*'s officers . . . ten of them to be precise. Which is a little awkward for you, perhaps. Because it means that once we have exchanged them for those of our own crew which you hold, then you *have* no guarantee of safe conduct left, do you . . . ?'

I couldn't help the vacant way in which I stared back at him. Probably not any more than the sardonic, victorious grin which he shone back at me.

And the perhaps understandable way in which he added softly, '. . . so how's *that*, *Herr Kapitän* – for a double stalemate?'

9

I didn't like it.

In fact that was probably the understatement of the year 1941. And it wasn't only the way this futile stalemate between us and the raider was progressing – or rather stagnating. As far as my earlier one-upmanship was concerned I was now left holding only the one card again, and that was likely to burn up in a mile-high ball of exploding ammunition the minute we cleared the narrow channel.

But the worry of more immediate concern was the impending exchange of prisoners, and there were several unsettling facets to *that* risky operation.

First and foremost, I just couldn't bring myself to trust the *Seepanther*. I'd seen her in action, remember, and while it was hard to view that traumatic event with an unbiased eye I still believed she could have offered us some aid, some support before she left us to burn or drown, despite the smooth *Kapitänleutnant* Flindt's protestations. Because whatever they claimed, the fact was that Timmer's gun had been knocked out while they were still within visual distance . . . they could have returned without the slightest threat to their own safety.

Unless they really were fighting the most savage kind of sea war – a total war. Where survivors were at best an irrelevant nuisance, at worst a doctrinaire target . . .

And secondly there was the fact that we were completely unarmed – apart from that bloody gun of Timmer's. For close-order repelling of boarders we had nothing, not even a flare pistol. And Flindt *knew* that – he'd even remarked on it as he rejoined his boat after our first unprofitable parley. 'No tricks during the exchange, mind.' I'd warned with all the threatening power of a toothless bulldog. He'd hesitated a moment, gazing round at the *Maya Star*'s piratical crew holding a variety of brickbats and stopper chains, and then turned back to me with a look of intense seriousness. 'Our German sailors would not dare, *Herr Kapitän*. In case you beat them severely – with marline spikes and ropes' ends, hah?'

Just before he'd climbed down the ladder. Chuckling all the way to his launch.

But perhaps the most perturbing and the most risky part of the forthcoming exchange was that our solitary natural defence would have to be compromised – the high, vertical freeboard of the *Maya Star*'s towering hull. That formidable obstacle was enough to deter any surprise attack and, allied to the vulnerability of ship's boats to assorted heavy objects dropped from above, at least afforded us a certain security. Only now I would be forced to allow ten men – ten unknown men who might be British or might simply be the fertile products of an enterprising *Kapitänleutnant's* imagination – to board the decks of my ship, because I knew I had no alternative but to try to help them.

If they were genuine survivors!

I made a firm resolution to make damned sure I *was* sure, before one strange foot stepped across the *Star*'s bulwarks.

But I still felt all cold and uneasy inside. When I saw the crowded launch approaching from a warship which I knew, deep down in my heart, just had to kill us to be really secure herself . . .

The *Seepanther*'s boat held a crew of only two ratings. I'd stipulated that as a maximum with Flindt before agreeing to the exchange. She also carried the man who would be the first to board the *Maya Star* – the senior surgeon from the raider who would inspect, and supervise the transfer of the wounded Germans. More importantly to me, he also intended to treat our own injured crewmen before he left, as well as furnish a basic medical kit for our hopefully outward passage.

And then there were the survivors from the *Wellington*

149

Court – the alleged British Merchant Navy officers themselves . . .

I watched tightly as the boat drew alongside. There were
ten of them, just as Flindt had promised. Ten men wearing a
motley assortment of clothing ranging from smart reefer
jackets and caps to one rigged in pyjama trousers, seaboots
and a porkpie hat. I moved over to the Bosun, waiting at the
top of the ladder with a somewhat ostentatious and very
heavy slab of concrete balanced warningly on the bulwark.

'What d'you think of 'em?' I whispered doubtfully.

He shrugged, gazing keenly into the boat. 'Could be
British, I s'ppose. Or Irish or Swedes f'r that matter,
Cap'n.'

'Or Jerries,' I muttered pensively. One of the younger
men in the launch, a fair-haired lad wearing the purple-
backed lace of a third engineer on his sleeve, grinned up at
us and called, 'Bloody glad to see you chaps. Decent of you
to do this for us.'

'*Chaps* . . . ?' Fletcher growled suspiciously. 'I 'aven't
never 'eard no British sailor sayin' *chaps*. Not never!'

'He's got educashun,' Chippie countered from further
along. 'You never 'eard it 'cause no one wi' educashun ever
spoke to you, Bosun.'

'Stop it you two,' I snapped nervously, scanning the up-
turned faces for something, anything, to help me understand what lay in the minds of those supposed comrades.
But all I saw was an even more unsettling blankness, a sort
of general wariness . . . or was it apathy. Had their capture
and subsequent treatment dulled what might have been
expected to be a more exuberant anticipation of release?

Or did they know something that I didn't? As yet.

I wasn't in the mood for the conventions of politeness so I
merely nodded a curt acknowledgement as the *Kreigsmarine*
surgeon swung up the pilot ladder. 'Take this officer to the
saloon, Mister Ainslie,' I ordered. 'Gifford's waiting for
him there.'

The first hostage placed his foot on the ladder until I

shouted 'Belay that! Which of you is the master?'

It may have been my overworked imagination but they seemed to be momentarily taken aback, then a heavy-set man stood up in the boat and looked up at me. He was wearing a tweed sports jacket over navy blue serge trousers and was bareheaded.

'Here! Captain Trueman, *Wellington Court*, Mister.'

I glanced at the Bosun. The man below had a heavy Lancashire accent yet there was something abrupt, something not quite natural in the way he spoke.

'I'm Barton, acting captain . . . What line are you with, Captain?'

'Wellington Shipping Company, Liverpool. Thee should know that thyself, lad.'

I ignored the implied rebuke. 'Where d'you live? What address?'

'Derby Road, Bootle . . . Number four eighty-two.'

'What bus would you catch to get from home to the centre of Liverpool . . . say to Kendal Milne's department store in Deansgate?'

This time there was a very positive silence, until Trueman growled tightly, 'You playing silly buggers, Mister . . . ? I'd get a tram f'r a start. But 'appen I'd not be goin' into t'Pool for Kendal Milne, I'd be setting course for Manchester . . . On't *train* dammit!'

And then gradually, as the point of the questions sank in, the captain's face became more and more suffused while he broke into the most colourful, foc'sle-inspired tirade of Anglo-Saxon swearing I'd ever heard outside of an argument between Fletcher and the Carpenter. And when the man in the boat had finally ground to a halt through sheer lack of breath I glanced at the Bosun to meet a broad grin.

'Well, he's British,' Fletcher confirmed with enormous respect. 'That one's as British as a wet bank 'oliday, Mister B.'

'Welcome aboard, Cap'n,' I called in relief. 'We don't have roast beef but by God we can offer you a cup o' tea.'

But even then only one man laughed – the young third engineer who'd spoken earlier. The rest of them just smiled a little vaguely while the florid Captain Trueman positively glared round him with what almost seemed like anger. In fact as I stood back from the bulward to allow the first man access to the *Maya Star*'s deck I found it strangely difficult to summon even a nod of greeting . . . there was still that remoteness about the whole event, still something not quite right.

Quickly I stepped alongside Fletcher. 'Watch them,' I whispered uneasily. 'Pass it along, every man on his toes!'

And saw from the way the Bosun caressed the concrete block poised above that launch, and from the manner in which the rest of our crew gripped their makeshift weapons, that I wasn't alone in my mistrust.

But none of us were even remotely prepared for what *did* happen, not even then. Not even resigned as we were to the unexpected in that place which already reeked of dead things . . .

The *Wellington Court*'s third engineer was the first stranger inboard. He dropped lightly to the deck and grinned that cheerful, slightly rueful grin again. 'Thanks,' he said gratefully. 'You really put one over on Jerrie this time, Sir.'

But as I said, I only threw a curt nod and snapped, 'Over there, Mister. Where we can see you.'

The second man came over the rail wearing the three rings of a chief officer. 'Name?' I probed. He blinked at me and muttered equally sharply, 'Smith . . . Bill Smith.'

'Smith?' I wondered bitterly, 'or Schmidt . . . ?' but they were coming aboard fast now, anxiously, one after the other, and I began to feel crowded with the unease turning into an outright apprehension. Yet there was Captain Trueman still below in the launch and I'd have sworn he was as genuine as any Lancashire lad could be.

But suddenly, it seemed, there were six *Wellington Court* men already on deck with the rest of them strung out on the pilot ladder and climbing urgently, purposefully . . .

'HOLD IT . . . !' I roared as the panic suddenly over-took logic. 'No one else across that rail until . . .'

Only I was too late. As usual I was far too bloody late to keep control of events which had a disconcerting habit of building into crisis with a crazily escalating momentum . . . and to come from what appeared to be several different directions at *once* f'r Chrissake!

From Third Mate Ainslie, for instance . . . abruptly running towards us along the promenade deck with Gifford following. And both of them waving their arms and shouting something totally incomprehensible about '. . . ber-serk! Look out f'r yourselves 'cause he's coming down . . .'

And then at the same moment, the master of the *Welling-ton Court* from the bottom of the pilot ladder, in a voice suddenly completely out of control and with all the fury of a storm force ten.

'. . . Damned if I will . . . WATCH them bastards, *Maya Star*! Don't thee lettem get set to . . .'

'I knew it,' I heard myself blurting as I swung to face those alien newcomers. There was an unmistakable warning in that roar from the river, a warning issued with the pent-up release of a previously simmering volcano . . . But what the hell did *Ainslie* have to shout about though? What *other* blood-chilling horror was loose aboard the *Maya Star* on that nerve-rending, sunshine-washed deck?

Only there wasn't any more time left for speculation. Not when Able Seaman Ricketts – normally so slow and lugubrious – abruptly leapt forward with a scream of 'Watch out, Sir! He's got a . . .'

There was a sudden movement – a deafening report . . .

And Ricketts had fallen back to lie on the deck with a gaping, black-ringed hole in his chest and a look of terrible concentration on his face while he tried to mouth the last word of his existence.

'. . . gun . . .' the dying seaman whispered. Before the blood came out of his mouth and all the light went out of his still-open eyes.

While the man holding the Luger pistol – a man briefly known to me as Bill Smith, Chief Officer – snarled sharply, '*Schnell, SCHNELL! Schlag die Bastar . . .*'

Yet even during that raging moment when the two groups fell on each other in a cursing, pummelling mass of swaying bodies I was still aware of Ainslie's panic-stricken shouts from the deck above.

And realized with a blood-chilling certainty of horror, that he still wasn't warning us about the enemy already among us.

But that there was a greater terror – some other even more monstrous threat – also prowling the decks of the *Maya Star*.

I suppose that extraordinary situation of one thing happening immediately on another worked for, as well as against us. It certainly meant the raider's camouflaged boarding party were caught off-balance even more than the already suspicious crew of my own ship. But even then the suddenness of Rickett's slaying, and the way a well-trained squad of professional fighting men were geared to turn surprise into a tactical asset was enough to overwhelm us before we got into our stride.

They never got as far drawing their weapons though. Apart from Smith, or Schmidt, not one German sailor was given time to drag his automatic from concealment . . . the rest of that brief little war was spent in a flailing mêlée of fists, boots, marline spikes and teeth. The enemy crewmen borne on a tight, disciplined wave of grim determination while the *Maya Star*'s crowd just roared into the fray with a too-long-suppressed desire to hit back, to lash out viciously at the shadow which had hung over us for so many days.

I remember seeing Bosun Fletcher give the block of concrete one hefty, satisfying shove clean over the wall and through the bottom of the waiting launch before swinging towards the struggling mass and positively launching himself like a crash-landing seaplane . . . Then Chippie, mouthing obscenities, gripping a German sporting a second mate's rings in one enormous paw while battering the man's head mercilessly with the other clenched fist. Until a second *Kreigsmarine* commando kicked the old man vengefully in the kidneys and Chippie went down with a scream of agony . . .

'The GUN,' I was roaring. 'Get the bastard with the *gun* . . .'

Hotchkiss now, boring in from the engine room entrance with a look of absolute euphoria on his shiny black features . . . stamping hard on the face of a man in chief engineer's uniform already sprawled brokenly on deck – but that must've pleased Hotchkiss, doing that. Even if the bastard *was* only pretending to be a chief . . . A second *Seepanther* leaping on to the little greaser's back and holding him for his oppo to get the boot in . . . Hotchkiss still struggling on a spitting crescendo of gutter vituperation though, whirling round and round with superhuman strength before hurling the man from his back clean over the bulwarks and down towards the already threshing, drowning crew of the sinking launch.

Then a third German slamming a hardwood batten across Hotchkiss's own face, and the greaser skidding across the baking deck in a spray of blood and bits of tooth . . . Fletcher going down too now, roaring like a mad bull with three of the enemy on top of him . . . Another unfamiliar figure suddenly joining battle – a big man with a florid face . . . Trueman, by God! Captain Trueman of the *Wellington Court* now doing more than prove how British he was by the way he was smashing a blond Teutonic skull repeatedly against a fire hydrant and bellowing, 'Force *me* to be a bloody Judas, would thee? Hold my lads under the gun, would thee, so's I'd be forced to . . .'

But then he, too, vanished under a snarling pack of bodies and suddenly, ominously, I felt the prickle of disaster in the small of my back.

I kneed my own anonymous adversary in the groin and swung round abruptly. But there wasn't anyone left to help me . . . Ainslie and Gifford hadn't had time to reach the forward deck yet while Timmer and his skeleton crew were still aft, keeping a justifiably mistrustful watch on that threatening stretch of river. And even when our sadly depleted crew *did* manage to arrive, all they'd find waiting for them was the barrel of an equally deadly, if much smaller gun . . a Luger pistol, in fact . . .

Like the one staring at *me* from a range of three feet, f'r Christ's SAKE!

And I could tell from the look of barely-controlled rage on Chief Officer . . . or was it *Kapitänleutnant* Wilhelm Schmidt's bruised face that he would be more than de-lighted to use it.

Given just one, microscopic excuse – like my refusing to surrender the *Maya Star*. Within, say, the next five seconds.

I remember feeling the hopelessness swamping me in great trembling waves. And looking wildly around the decks of the ship we'd fought so long to save.

At the wreckage and the charred timbers. And the shell-splintered planking and the blasted remains of our once-proud superstructure.

And then I came across the men sprawled in unsightly, broken attitudes around me . . . Fletcher, still trying doggedly to drag himself to his knees while two German sailors waited above him for the first sign of a return to the fight. Chippie, moaning and clawing at the deck with agony . . . Hotchkiss spitting blood and oaths in equal proportions . . . the strange Captain Trueman . . . and Ricketts. Poor fumbling Ricketts with his eyes even more blank and vague than they'd ever been . . .

I heard the sound of footsteps running towards us, still out of sight in the starboard alleyway, but I knew they were too late to turn the tide as all the hatred and the fear and the sadness in me welled to the surface.

'BASTAAAAAAARDS!' I roared uncontrollably.

Just before I ground to a petrified, disbelieving halt. Along with every other man, friend or enemy, on that open, blood-spattered stretch of deck.

When from round the corner, as if clawed straight from a mad man's nightmare, the Devil himself shrieked towards us.

With the screaming, foam-flecked maw wide open. And a razor-sharp fire axe swinging in great flashing arcs above eyes which held a ghastly, homicidal promise . . .

I never did find out whether Smith, or Schmidt, would have pulled that Luger trigger and firmly – if somewhat irrelevantly by then – established whether Ricketts had been killed during a necessary act of war, or simply as the first victim in a coldly premeditated intention to dispose of all the *Muyu Star*'s crew.

But that had been the trouble with the *Seepanther* incident. Every single event to date had been a fuzzed and unspecific enigma, where it just wasn't possible to decide on the true motive, the real intent behind the actions of our enemy.

Even now, with our own resistence finally overwhelmed by weight of numbers, I was aware of a resentful gratitude for the Germans' taut self-restraint. As soon as the hectic mêlée collapsed the *Seepanther*'s boarders – who for sheer boot-in-the-gut brawling ability had to command our undisguised respect – had held themselves in tight check. But were they motivated by a genuine compunction, or was the momentary hesitation simply a disciplined wait for Schmidt's order before completing an act of total war.

Either way, whatever their reasons for delaying, and whatever tactics they'd been keyed to anticipate in the way of resistance, they could never, never, have been prepared for the horrific spectacle now avalanching upon them . . .

Did I say *they* hadn't been prepared, f'r crying out loud? Because personally I'd never been so terrified in all my life.

It bore in on the high-pitched scream of all the devils incarnate, that creature – that crazed apparition wielding the monstrous scything cleaver like some folk-lore bloody-bones from every man's most fevered deliriums.

We all swung in shock, even the furious Schmidt, but for sheer instant reflexes, my own battered crowd were top of the class. Hotchkiss literally scrabbled backwards along the deck with a frantic disregard for his earlier injuries . . . I saw Fletcher's bowed head snapping upwards in blank disbelief before he crawled on his hands and knees for safety, and Chippie dragging his hands from his agonized back to clamp them firmly around his head instead, abruptly galvanized into a rolling dive for the protection of the hatch coaming . . .

'*Mein Gott!*' somebody uttered in a shattered croak.

'Oh Gawd!' Hotchkiss was spitting through a retreating haze of gore.

But then the Thing was on us. I saw the axe arcing sideways and across while a frozen blonde head dissolved in a hideous mass of exploding, glistening shrapnel . . . Schmidt began swinging with the Luger rising and I, God help me, yelling dementedly, 'GETTIT, Mister . . . Oh f'r pity's sake shoot it down!'

A second already-dead victim spinning like a top before collapsing. The Thing altering course now, heading straight *for* me as I willed my legs to move, to run, to do any bloody thing which would drag me clear of that nightmare.

Bedlam! Men scattering frantically in every direction. Ainslie and Gifford seemingly doing exactly the reverse, though – literally falling towards me down the ladder and looking, at the same time, strangely grim and determined, not terror-stricken like the rest of us . . .

A report from beside me as the Luger slammed deafeningly. Then again, and again . . . and again. Only the creature *still* wouldn't stop, not even when bright red flowers splayed obscenely against the hurtling bulk . . .

Slam!

Another man screaming piercingly, clutching at a partly severed and arterial-spouting thigh, but the *Kreigsmariners* trying to re-form now, dragging at awkwardly concealed guns while attempting to make a stand . . . But only the three of them left upright – Schmidt plus the oddly attired one in pyjamas and a porkpie hat, and the young fair-haired German in third engineer's rig.

Slam . . . Slam! More flowers . . . more blood. But *still* comin' in f'r . . .

Porkpie and *erzatz* Third diving low, going for the creature's legs with enormous courage . . . Only Ainslie was also flying in too, with Gifford hard on his quarter, but the way they slammed into the two enemy boarders seemed a hell of an odd way to go about forming a truce . . .

'Please . . . *NOOOOOoooo* . . .'

The red glinting axe-head finally flailing in a wide sweep, zipping past my eyes by the thickness of a skin of paint . . . grey paint? Schmidt swinging away in desperation too, the terror of hopelessness finally dawning on his bruised features.

I closed my eyes. Tightly.

There was a blood-freezing gurgle. Immediately following the most sickening thud . . .

I kept my eyes shut for quite a long time after both men had toppled clean across the bulwarks and over the wall, carried outboard by the impetus of the crazed attack.

But I already knew that Ainslie and Gifford were well able to cope with the demoralized survivors from the *Seepanther*'s party. You see, they'd had a bit more time than the rest of us to catch up with the situation, to realize that it hadn't really been the work of a Thing or a creature or a devil, that appalling carnage of the last few seconds.

It had only been a quiet, ordinary sailorman actually. But with a shell splinter tormenting his brain.

Seaman Sproat. Lately of the Motor Vessel *Maya Star*.

It took me a few more minutes to catch up.

As usual I was grimly attempting to re-plan after the event, hindsight instead of anticipation. And while I stood there on that charnel house of a foredeck, with the sun slowly lowering against the back-drop of the jungle, I could feel a new determination growing in me as I watched first aid being administered to those latest casualties – friend and enemy – to be added to our growing list.

The raider's surgeon was a very busy man. He was a very uncomfortable man as well, come to that, but then again he did work for Hitler – it was perhaps a bit unreasonable to have expected the *Herr Doktor* to have compromised the surprise attack planned by his comrades-in-arms.

Still, we did our best to make sure his patriotic conscience didn't come under any further strain. The German automatic pistol Gifford held on him must have been a great incentive to concentrate on offering succour and not to worry too much about how the war was going. In fact my mind was so jaundiced after our latest clash with the *Seepanther* I'd even assumed the doctor was to blame in some way for poor Sproat's brief but gory rampage, at least until I'd heard the full story.

But the maddened seaman had simply slipped out of the saloon while the other wounded, including Steward Thomson, were receiving what Gifford affirmed later was impeccable attention from *Herr Doktor*. Probably we would never know whether Sproat had been selectively patriotic during the kill-crazy nightmare – or would he have gone for his shipmates too, had any of us happened to get in the way of that ghastly, flailing axe . . . ?

I shuddered. This wasn't a war any longer, it was deteriorating into a stalemate limbo of nerve-shredding horror. Unless I could do something, make *some* move which would end the suffering.

Or even the *Maya Star*. One way or another.

But before I could make any decision on our next action I had to weigh the facts.

Thomson, apparently, did still have a slim chance of

survival, according to the Second Cook. He'd received treatment which at least gave him a fifty-fifty prospect of coming out of this alive – but only *if* we could sail with him to a hospital within the next few hours, or . . .

'Or what, Gifford?' I said sharply.

He shrugged. 'Or we send 'im up to the sickbay aboard Jerrie, Sir. They got proper facilities there. An operatin' theatre an' that.'

I turned and stared back up the river, out past Timmer and Sparks still waiting by the poop gun. But there was nothing to be seen, no movement of any kind from the enemy, and in a few hours it would be too dark to keep any form of efficient watch, to have any warning of a second clandestine attempt to board.

Unless . . .

I swung back towards the master of the *Wellington Court* who stood bruised but unbowed. 'How many of your crew do they really hold aboard the *Seepanther*, Cap'n?'

'Just three. Yon Flindt was an opportunist, claimin' ten so's they could smuggle a larger party aboard thee . . . and happen I owe you an apology, Mister. I went along wi' them so far, but I couldn't keep it up in the end – not even with my own lads' safety at stake.'

'It didn't matter, not as it turned out,' I said shortly. But I already knew precisely how hard it must have been for him because Captain Trueman had also found himself choosing between his own personal Devil and that deep blue sea. Only there wasn't time for mutual commiseration, not until I'd assessed the odds against us.

'If you're hoping to make a deal with 'em, watch it,' Trueman tendered cautiously. 'There's some of 'em on that raider are harder-line Nazis than Goebbels. That little bastard over there wearin' third engineer's rings, the one that talks posh English. He's a proper fanatical little Jew-baiter f'r a start.'

Bleakly I eyed the group of sullen captives tied to the ladder and couldn't help, at the same time, noticing the look of triumph which Bosun Fletcher directed at Chippie. 'Well *he's* off their team for the moment,' I commented sourly. 'What about the rest – what about their Old Man for instance?'

'Old school German Navy, I'd say. Cold as ice, but made damn sure my crew were adequately provisioned before leaving them in the boats.'

'We thought for a while they'd machine-gunned you.'

He grinned tightly. 'Happen I wouldn't be here in that case. No, they only took me along wi' my first, second and fourth mates because we couldn't hide the fact we were wearing officers' whites. All the engineers from the Chief down looked like bloody tauregs anyway, an' none of the crowd would let on which they were.'

I chewed my lip moodily. Every new piece of information I gained about the *Seepanther*'s captain seemed to cancel out the one before. I was as far away from understanding his real character as I'd ever been.

'Yet the same man sanctioned a pretty underhanded bluff to take over this ship. And damn nearly succeeded!'

Trueman looked at me pityingly. 'Aren't thee talking like a lad wet behind the ears, Mister? Look, he's the skipper of a lone-wolf commerce raider. Subterfuge is his tool o' trade, both to kill ships an' avoid being killed by bigger ships. It's the only way he can fight efficiently – to hit hard, fast *and* sneaky if the occasion demands it . . . And yon *Seepanther*'s captain is a master craftsman, both thee an' me knows it. Too bloody well!'

'Then you're telling me *not* to trust his word. That he'll go for us the moment we're clear of the narrow channel whatever we do.'

'I'm telling you the nature of the beast. And any beast gets more dangerous, more unpredictable when he's cornered. And happen he could get vindictive, too. God help us and any other British merchantman who runs across him once he's free again.'

And that was . . . well . . . that. My dilemma as before. If we stayed, the *Seepanther* would inevitably be forced into a further attempt to board us, yet if we left our only safe anchorage then she'd probably sink us anyway, before we'd even steamed a mile out to sea . . .

. . . while there was another factor which I hadn't even considered until this moment. And that was what would happen later, to other ships, when my *Maya Star* had finally been battered into a foundering, exploding hulk. Because Trueman was right – the *Seepanther* only existed for one reason, to run amok among the Allied supply routes of the South Atlantic. It could be weeks, even months before the Navy finally ran her to ground and sank her. Months . . . and a lot of broken ships. A bobbing trail marked by hosts of mutilated seaman . . .

I stood glowering helplessly at the obscenely twisted corpses still huddled on the *Maya Star*'s deck, and feeling the sick frustration and the fear for my own crew rising even more bitterly than before. Until, suddenly, my eyes fell on the group of German captives again, and something Trueman had just said took on a new significance.

'Subterfuge . . . the only way he can fight efficiently . . .'

Because everything that plagued me, every threat to my own ship and crew, could actually apply *both* ways, couldn't it?

My ship carried over two thousand *tons* of ammunition, enough to supply two warships like the *Seepanther*. And that meant that the only real difference between us was that she had the means of delivering her part of that horrific blasting power, whereas the *Maya Star* didn't.

Or not until now, anyway. For Trueman had suddenly given me the answer to that problem, too.

By the one measure which was common to both ships . . .

I swung abruptly. I was sick of the fear generated by what a *warship* might or might not do when backed into a corner. Maybe, just maybe it was time for the weak to become outraged, for the little men to break a few humanitarian precepts.

Little men like us. On an insignificant little ship. Like the *Maya Star*.

'Mister Ainslie,' I snarled, so savagely that the Third Mate almost sprang to attention.

'Sir.'

'Have the motor boat made ready immediately. And while I'm gone, get hold of Bombardier Timmer – there are certain preparations I want you to make . . .'

'*Gone*, Sir?'

I smiled, but with a terrible burning rage inside me. 'To visit the *Seepanther*, Mister. Because – just for a bloody change – *we* are declaring Total War . . . On a warship.'

10

It would have been hard to decide which were the palest things in evidence in the motor boat by the time it drew alongside the *Seepanther*'s lowered accommodation ladder – our limpid truce flag or the complexions of Seaman Cleese and myself. But anger can evaporate very quickly during a short river passage, when all you're sure of is that there are three hundred displeased enemies waiting for you at the end of it.

Probably the most nerve-racking moment of all was when we finally cleared the bend and saw the raider for the second time that day. I remember that the first thing to flash across my mind was the impression that she wasn't even making any attempt to hide her true origin any longer, presumably from the chance eyes of any educated local inhabitants – because now the German Swastika flew aggressively unashamed from the warship's counter.

Or ominously perhaps, in our case. As if indicating that the time of the velvet glove was rapidly drawing to a close as far as they were concerned as well . . . I swallowed and gestured to Cleese at the tiller. 'Take us alongside the companionway. Stay with the boat if you can but, if they order you aboard, just go with 'em. And for God's sake don't get all bolshie an' unco-operative. Right?'

He glanced up at the *Seepanther*'s looming bridge wing, and at the two white-uniformed ratings standing alertly beside her machine-gun, and muttered apprehensively, 'Cap'n, you gotter be *jokin*'!'

I forced a weak smile and hoped he'd be all right – or was this fated to be another of my immaculately conceived plans ending in total disaster, in a P.O.W. camp at best if only part of my approach went wrong. I began to feel more than glad that I'd only allowed one volunteer to accompany me on this visit to the lion's – or was it the wolf's? – lair. Not that I could see much hope for Ainslie or Fletcher or Chippie or any of the others still aboard the *Maya Star* anyway, not if I failed this time . . .

. . . and then we were sheering alongside the bottom of the raider's ladder platform where two more uniformed but, I noticed with relief, unarmed seamen were waiting to take our bow rope. Nobody warned us off, and nobody shot at us.

But then again, nobody knew precisely why I'd come, either.

Or at least not yet.

I conveyed a last hopefully reassuring nod to Cleese, and stepped on to the ladder. The German rating nearest came to smart attention and gestured upwards. '*Bitte.*'

I didn't give him more than a curt acknowledgement. It wasn't acting a part or anything, I simply couldn't trust myself to speak right then, not after having cleared the first hurdle and found myself still alive. I began to climb what seemed a very long way, and all the time a little voice in my head kept nagging, 'Keep it cool, Barton. Remember you're playing a dangerous game, chum . . .'

But I'd heard *that* little voice before. Which was why I was having to climb this bloody ladder in the first place.

They were waiting for me at the top – the familiar aquiline features of *Kapitänleutnant* Flindt backed by a whiter-than-white petty officer of some sort and the apparently inevitable duo of wooden-faced ratings. These two did have weapons, uncompromising-looking submachine-guns, but at least they remained angled across their chests as the lower deck ramrodded to attention.

Flindt stepped forward and saluted stiffly. '*Kapitän.*'

I noticed grimly that he didn't look right at me this time, just kept his eyes fixed impassively on a point somewhere a long way behind my shoulder, and couldn't help wondering spitefully whether protocol or guilt dictated such a formal reception.

And then I forgot all about the good advice my little voice had given me on that ladder as I heard myself saying bitterly, 'Would you like to shoot me this way, Lieutenant? Or shall I turn round so's you can do it in the back?'

Which was a great curtain-raiser, even for a psuedo-diplomatic negotiation.

His stare didn't falter. Only a throbbing pulse in the side of his neck gave any indication of real feeling. 'You refused our offer of safe conduct for your crew, Sir. Consequently, according to the rules of war you left yourselves open to unrestricted retaliation.'

I was glad he'd said that. It proved we were all thinking along the same lines.

'You have five more dead and one badly wounded shipmate to question how wide open we did leave ourselves, Mister,' I retorted coldly. I didn't add that it had taken a madman from the Devil's pit to restore the balance, but he did look at me then, just for a moment.

'Willy Schmidt?' he asked hesitantly.

'Their leader? Oh, I though his name was Smith . . . Bill Smith,' I said looking all surprised.

'Please. It is important for me to know, *Kapitän*.'

'Well, he's dead, Mister,' I offered brutally. 'As dead as another man called Able Seaman Ricketts . . .'

And then I hesitated abruptly. Because for the first time I detected a reaction in the young German officer's eyes that I'd already seen too often. An expression of sadness, and of pain for what might have been.

'He was the husband of my sister, and my very close friend,' the boy said in a dull, low voice.

But that only honed the anger in me to a finer edge. I didn't want to believe we had anything in common, not even grief, so I just shrugged – the same gesture he'd displayed a little earlier, on learning of the death of Jeremy Prethero.

'Like you said yourself, Flindt – war can be a hard taskmaster. Only that can apply to the men who stand behind the guns, too. Maybe you should remember that next time.'

The remoteness shuttered over his eyes again and he swung abruptly. 'You will please follow me. My captain is expecting you in his quarters.'

I took a deep breath and stepped from the head of the gangway to the well-scrubbed decks of the *Seepanther*. There wasn't any blood to mar them as there was on the scarred timbers of the *Maya Star*.

But anything was possible. Especially when one side or another was pressurized a little too far, was virtually forced to dispense with even the basic rules of war. Like I was currently attempting to do.

The only snag being that I had an unsettling premonition that the *Seepanther* had also reached that stage.

Now, it seemed, the only unknown factor would be . . . well . . . which side was going to dispense with them first.

Flindt stepped to one side and slammed erect as I brushed aggressively past him and into the cabin. But there was only my calculated determination now, any fear had gone as soon as I passed the point of no return.

'*Kapitän* Barton of the *Maya Star* . . . Herr *Korvetten-kapitän* Neugard.'

The man standing behind the desk didn't look at all as I'd expected. Of rather less than medium build he seemed a little too fat, a little too florid – but then he glanced towards me and I could feel the vigour in his appraisal while the steely expression belied any suggestion of softness. He didn't waste time with formalities.

'You have brought your papers – secret papers?'

I blinked at the suddenness of the attack, then thought, 'O.K., Korvetten-whoever, if that's the way you want to play it . . .'

'I'll have to send for some. Are you short of tobacco too, Mister?'

It was Neugard's turn to blink. '*Wie bitte?* What are you saying?'

I matched his look of mystification. 'I though you were asking for cigarette papers, Captain. Weren't you?'

For a moment he continued his penetrating stare then, slowly, he allowed the suspicion of a smile to crease the corners of his mouth. There wasn't all that much humour in it, though.

'Then I can assume that you have *not* come to surrender your ship, Captain Barton?'

'You assume correctly.'

He shrugged. 'Then I must also assume that I cannot brow-beat you, while I have the distinct feeling that I would be equally foolish to suggest that there is no room for . . . ah . . . diplomatic immunity aboard the *Seepanther*, and that you might now be a prisoner of the *Kriegsmarine*?'

'It would be a bit short-sighted, yes. Especially from your point of view.'

'May I ask why?'

'Because there are now explosive charges secured to the inlet valves of the *Mayu Star*. If I do not return within one hour my Third Officer has been ordered to detonate them, Captain – and your *Seepanther* will remain sealed in this bloody backwater until the bottom rusts out've her. *Verstehen?*'

'And you intend, no doubt, to threaten precisely the same action should any further attempts be made to board you, eh *Kapitän* Barton?'

I eyed him a little disconcertedly. 'Aye,' I replied shortly.

He nodded thoughtfully and, clasping his hands behind his back, walked over to the open scuttle and stared through it. 'Then I trust you have come to propose a solution to this . . . ah . . . impasse, have you not?'

I couldn't help feeling a little resentful. The conversation wasn't going at all as I'd planned it. But then again, neither had anything else up to now. I took a deep breath and plunged.

'I've come to give you advance notice, Neugard. That I will be sailing the *Maya Star* at midnight for the nearest safe haven.'

He didn't move for a moment but I could sense the stir of surprise, or was it outrage, from the silent Flindt behind me. Then the German captain turned again.

'Then you must realize that you may be dead before one-o-clock in the morning, Barton. That my mandate as the officer commanding this warship requires me to take every opportunity of destroying the enemies of the Third Reich.'

'And does that resolution apply to the *servants* of your Third Reich as well, Mister? Because I intend keeping your own men as hostages against our safe passage, and I promise you – they'll be secured right down in the bottom of my own ship. They'll be the first to die if she does sink.'

Neugard stared at me grimly. 'Using hostages as a defensive tactic is considered a direct contravention of the Geneva Agreement.'

'Probably it is,' I agreed equably. 'I suppose it could just be considered as outright murder, come to that . . . but you at least have the final decision on whether or not you pull the trigger.'

His eyes raked mine, searching for something. I hoped he would find it – it was very important that he did.

'If I give you my word on your conduct, will you return my men before you sail?'

'No.'

He didn't say anything right away, so I amplified with a shake of my head. 'I'd prefer to continue hostilities on a basis of mutual mistrust. I don't plan to test whether your loyalty to your *Führer* is stronger than your bond to the master of an enemy ship. I'm hanging on to my guarantees in the flesh, so to speak.'

'You realize that my surgeon commander is a non-combatant?'

'He sure as hell is one now. And so are your wounded, whether they like it or not. Unless . . .'

Neugard stared at me interrogatively. 'Unless what, *Kapitän*?'

'You still hold three officers from the *Wellington Court*. I am prepared to exchange them for your three most seriously wounded crewmen.'

'Why should I agree? Why should I exchange three healthy men for an equal number of sick?'

I grinned sardonically. 'Actually I didn't expect them to be all that healthy, Mister. Not after the threat you used against Cap'n Trueman to force him to add a little *bona fides* to your boarding party.'

This time Neugard did look irritable to say the least. 'I am *not* a Naz . . .' Then he became aware of Flindt watching covertly and altered course abruptly. 'I may threaten with them, but I do not make war with hostages, *Kapitän* Barton.'

'Well I've got to,' I countered succinctly. 'Seein' I don't have a battery of six-inch guns to employ as an alternative. Do you want your blokes or not?'

The raider captain hesitated. I could see from the way he chewed his lower lip savagely that he was a man torn between loyalties and felt a stirring, if not exactly of sympathy, then at least of fellow-feeling as I appreciated once again how narrow the real dividing line between us was – and that *Korvettenkapitän* Neugard, just as I had done, could also find himself torn irresolutely between his own personal Devil and that deep blue sea of doubt.

'What about my other men? Do you seriously expect me to allow you to hand them over for internment and do nothing to stop you?'

I pretended to consider momentarily. 'All right. Then you provide me with an extra boat and a chart. When I have covered, say, thirty miles towards safety I shall leave them afloat at a prearranged position for you to recover . . . By the way, where *is* the nearest port for me to head for, with hospital facilities?'

'You demand a lot, *Herr Kapitän* Barton.'

But he didn't sound bitter, only warily respectful. I shrugged. 'I *need* a lot. Both of us do, Mister ... and we can only get it by breaking the stalemate. After that it's up to you.'

For a moment longer Neugard eyed me grimly, then he nodded abruptly. 'Very well, *Kapitän*, I agree to your suggestion. *Herr* Flindt will brief you on whatever navigational information you require, and arrange transfer of the three hostages each way ...'

'Not like last time, eh?' I probed cautiously. He shook his head. '*Nein*. But there is one thing you must know, my friend ...'

I raised my eyebrow queryingly as the German captain continued in a low, very emphatic tone.

'... your nearest refuge lies south of here. If, for any reason you appear to deviate from your previously agreed track to the point where my men are to be left – then I will be watching. And the *Seepanther* will catch you, and kill you all, my own men included if necessary. *Verstehen, Kapitän?*'

And I *verstehen'd* only too clearly.

'Give me two hours,' I growled. 'Two hours to get clear.'

His eyes held mine for a long moment. Then he shrugged. 'Very well! But I warn you that the *Seepanther* will be moving down river to your present anchorage as you sail. When I reach it I will stop ... but I shall watch you, *Kapitän* Barton. Watch you very closely indeed.'

I said, 'Oh, aye?' calmly. And hoped he wouldn't detect the dismay in my expression. You see, that wasn't part of the plan – or not part of *my* plan, anyway. Not for the raider to delay for two hours in the area the *Maya Star* had so recently vacated. Because the concentration of a look-out invariably weakens over that period of time, and eyes begin to roam idly, to probe the surrounding blackness, and to notice things not apparent at first glance ...

... but then again, it hadn't been a part of my planning

172

for Neugard to keep his word in the first place. I hadn't even seriously considered that possibility until then, but as I did so I felt doubly uneasy because I was firmly committed now to the totality of war and to killing *Korvettenkapitän* Neugard no matter what happened.

The snag was that I might have to place the *Maya Star* and her crew into an even greater hazard than before if the worst came to the worst – and Neugard eventually proved himself to be an embarrassingly honourable man.

There was little we could do between my return to the *Maya Star* and the onset of darkness. Except supervise – under the reassuring cover of our captured automatic weapons – the exchange of prisoners, and watch with understanding and maybe slightly wistful eyes as Trueman welcomed the three liberated officers from the *Wellington Court*.

We knew, Ainslie and Fletcher and Chippie and Cleese and the rest of us, that we could never meet with our own shipmates again. Not unless there really was a place for dead sailormen to greet old friends. A place we, ourselves, might very well be taken to before tomorrow grew very old . . .

But then the night did lay its concealing blanket over the poor decks of the *Maya Star*, and we set to work.

Oh, we'd done it once before – handling that ammunition which lay so sinister and evil in the quickly opened hatches. But never in total darkness, and never with a cold deliberation which required every ounce of a man's courage as opposed to that survival-inspired desperation which had spurred our earlier nightmare.

And then there was Timmer's specialist role, Bombardier Timmer whom I'd sworn was never to be allowed to come near an explosive device again as long as his built-in clumsiness hazarded my ship. Yet now I was allowing his earnest bespectacled features to frown in enormous concentration while he actually *armed* each individual, monstrous threat.

Fused over two hundred naval H.E. rounds for detonation on impact. In pitch darkness, in the middle of the night. In the middle of a swaying . . .

But I didn't want to think about that part of it. Not right at that moment.

Until finally we were finished. The freighter *Maya Star* was ready to sail to war again but this time, perhaps, as the hunter. Or was it the decoy? Whatever it was it marked yet another point of the agonizing voyage for me, because that was the time when I could have told my crew – could have warned them – about what I knew I had to do should *Korvettenkapitän* Neugard keep his word and allow us to escape.

But I didn't. I didn't have the courage to face them after all they'd been through, and to tell them about my own personal nightmare – about the ships that would die and the sailors who could choke their lives out under a carpet of fuel oil in the very near future if I didn't balance the survival of ourselves and the *Maya Star*, an already badly damaged ship and a very small number of lives, against ensuring that the *Seepanther* could never make any kind of war again.

Oh, they knew what was planned on the assumption that our enemy's war would be unrestricted, *would* be totally unscrupulous, and that Neugard intended to come after us as soon as we cleared the narrow channel. But to them the preparations we'd just completed had been a last resort, a form of desperate insurance against treachery.

And not one of the men facing me would ever know, until it was too late for discussion, that I intended to deliver our crazily-conceived weapon whatever happened . . .

I stirred myself, staring blankly for a moment at the faces of the men before me. It was too late now, too late for explanations and too early for apologies. I peered at my watch, luminous in the cloying night, and listened to the sounds of the jungle for the last time.

And then said quietly, 'Go on stand-by for sailing now, all of you. And may God go with each and every man aboard this ship tonight.'

To which Chippie added a subdued but deeply fervent 'Amen!'

And not even Bosun Fletcher disagreed with that.

I I

It was illogical, really. The way we kept our voices low, and even orders were given in whispers as if our sailing was a secret, clandestine affair instead of the declared gamble we were being forced to take.

It was equally illogical to imagine that the enemy would be out there, watching from the banks of that mist-shrouded river, because I knew that at this moment the crew of the *Seepanther* were as busily engaged as we were in preparing their ship for sea. But it still didn't prevent every man aboard the *Maya Star* casting anxious glances over rails or bulwarks from time to time with the ironic prayer that he *wouldn't* see anything in the black, sliding water that passed our flanks, that he wouldn't be able to detect the largest clumps of rotting vegetation which constantly drifted seawards on the slow outgoing current.

Because it was that impenetrable, non-reflective miasma that the jungle created during the small hours which was essential to our survival. Where shapes could only be seen when silhouetted against the fractionally lighter sky . . . so that a ship could be picked out at a distance of five miles or more, yet a hand held low down was virtually invisible, as if it didn't exist.

It was an eerie, lonely time to open a battle. But a very appropriate backdrop for a killing ground . . .

I stirred and walked to the after end of that skeletal bridge, gazing astern towards the shadowy Red Ensign which flew as defiantly as it had always done, and towards the steering position on the poop. Fletcher would be there, waiting at the wheel, along with the Chief Officer of the *Wellington Court*. There would be no need to feel our way out with the lead this time, the chart provided by Neugard was ready and illuminated by a shaded red torch held in Captain's Trueman's steady hand. It showed we had a fourteen hour run to a coastal settlement and safety if luck, and the *Seepanther*, allowed us the opportunity.

I knew Timmer and his gun crew were closed up and waiting down there, too. Waiting alertly and, perhaps in Bombardier Timmer's case, almost hopefully for an order to 'Fire. At will!' . . . and I'd underlined the word *order* with a bleak and totally unmistakable emphasis on this particular occasion.

Or was I being a little too cynical? Because Timmer thought, like everyone else, that I only intended to utter that martial absolution as a last resort and on a note of utter despair. And that it could mean that Timmer and everyone else aboard could be dead in the white hot space of a warship's anger later . . .

I glanced at my watch for the tenth time – two minutes to midnight. Swinging abruptly I walked to the front of the bridge as the Third Mate called quietly, 'Cable's up and down, Sir.'

'Aye, aye.'

I took the after-steering position field telephone from Apprentice Meehan. At least we were properly organized in that department now, with a seaman relaying through each line. 'All ready aft, Mister Hodgson?'

'All ready, Sir, when you are.' The ex-Chief Officer of the *Wellington Court* sounded cool as a cucumber.

I nodded in the darkness. 'Then midships the wheel, if you please.'

Above the splutter of interference I could hear Fletcher's gruff voice in the background. 'Wheel's midships, Sir . . .' then the acknowledgement into the handset itself . . . 'Wheel's amidships, Sir.'

A quick glance forward, out to where the glint of the sea waited masked only by the black flare of the *Maya Star*'s bows. The windlass still ground with a steady clank of incoming chain cable.

'Tell Mister Nolan to be ready for manoeuvring.'

Seaman Cleese on the other phone relayed the caution in a tone of controlled excitement. I wondered absently how the Second Engineer felt. Certainly he'd been able to move around his restricted kingdom a little easier since the *Herr Doktor* had treated those awful burns, but we still had to rely on him a lot as our only engineer. I hoped he would spend tomorrow night in hospital, both him and Steward Thomson . . .

'Anchor's aweigh, Sirrrrr . . .' from the foc'slehead.

'Aye, aye, Chippie.'

I took a deep breath.

'Dead slow ahead both engines, please.'

The deck began to throb immediately and, a few moments later, I could detect the skyline of the jungle starting to move slowly astern.

Trueman glanced up from the chart momentarily. The red wash from the torch threw his features into craggy relief.

'Here's to a safe voyage, Captain,' he said quietly.

But I didn't answer right away. I simply turned to face aft again, searching with the binoculars towards that still-vaguely detectable lighter patch which marked the bend in the river.

And then I stiffened.

'Aye,' I muttered. Very, very sincerely. Because there was a black, sinister shape just beginning to encroach on the gap astern, gradually looming against the jagged line of the jungle.

It told me that the *Seepanther* was on the move as well.

Fifteen minutes later and we were nearly clear of that sand spit stretching to seaward, now running out along our port side.

I stood with the fresh, clean sea wind caressing my face as the *Maya Star*'s bows began to lift to the first touch of the Atlantic swell, but I wasn't really conscious of it. Not at that moment. Because at any time now we would find out whether *Korvettenkapitän* Neugard was strong enough to hold back for the safety of his own men, or yield to the pressures of his calling – with the added knowledge that his failure to sink an already damaged *Maya Star* would risk the severe displeasure of the German High Command.

'Five minutes to your starboard turning point, Cap'n,' Trueman called.

'Thank you,' I said as matter-of-factly as I could. 'Half ahead both engines, Cleese.'

'Half ahead both engines, Sir.'

Ainslie came over and stood beside me. There was more reflected light from the wave facets out here and I could even detect the lines of his face, youthful as ever with the darkness masking the strain I knew was there.

'Can you still make her out – the raider?'

I shook my head. 'Not now. She just merges in with the shoreline . . . unless we can pick her out again as she shows up against that cliff face at the entrance.

'Or she opens fire,' the Third Mate muttered. 'We'll see her well enough then, by God!'

Glancing forward, towards the sea horizon, I noticed how the water glittered and sparkled in a wide periphery ahead, free of the drifting, enshrouding mist of the jungle. It struck me then that the *Seepanther*'s captain had been very perceptive in one thing.

'But she's able to see us all right,' I observed grimly. 'From a gunner's point of view we're standing out like a duck in a shooting gallery, Mister Ainslie.'

I didn't add the rest of it – that the angle between our present position and the *Seepanther*'s down-river heading meant she would be able to use every gun she carried, a full broadside if necessary. And I shuddered at the memory of what even her restricted fire power had done to us on that previous nightmare occasion.

'Two minutes,' Trueman called. 'Your new course is starb'd to sou' east by east, Captain. *If* we can lay any faith in yon compass Jerrie's provided down aft, mind.'

But it wasn't running aground that worried me right then. Ainslie lifted the binoculars, scanning the dimly seen entrance anxiously, as I shrugged, 'It doesn't matter. I wasn't planning to lose sight of land anyway, an' that's f'r sure . . .'

Then the Third Mate blurted, 'There she *is*!' and I was whirling astern and swallowing hard and grabbing for the binoculars all at the same time as Ainslie ended in a funny, almost hardly-daring-to-hope whisper, 'And I think she's stopped again, Sir. She's keeping to her word and letting us run for it.'

It must have been rather surprising, judging by the way they all stared at me in blank incomprehension, when I suddenly kicked the already battered bridge front in an agony of bitter frustration. Unwittingly the enemy had passed the initiative back to me. I couldn't help snarling obscurely, 'God save us all . . . from honourable men like Neugard!'

I knew the rest of the *Maya Star*'s crew had seen it too, the low silhouette of the *Seepanther* coming to rest precisely against the backdrop of that lighter shaded cliff face. I could tell that much by the sudden excited shout from aft, 'Jerrie's heavin'-to, lads. An' we're away an' fancy free . . .' And then the ragged cheering as men raced towards the poop, clinging to the grimly trained shape of the gun and just hanging out to pierce the gloom that lay between us and a rapidly fading nightmare.

But the cheering didn't last for long. Hardly a moment longer in fact, than the shocked, disbelieving silence which still reigned over the men surrounding me. Not when I hurried to the after end of the bridge and, leaning well over with cupped hands, roared, '*BELAY* THAT, damn you! TIMMER . . . Keep your gun crew closed UP, d'you hear.'

Just before Trueman said, in a slightly wary growl, 'What's biting thee, Mister? Dammit but you've pulled it off, lad. They're lettin' us go home . . .'

But now it really was too late. The Devil was mine, the deep blue sea which beckoned so enticingly was mine . . . and the responsibility would be all mine.

While the future years of living with a torment of self-hatred would be mine too. *If* I had any years left to live.

'What was the course agreed with Neugard, Captain?' I snapped urgently.

Even through the darkness I could sense the relief dawning in his eyes. 'Starboard. On to sou' east by east . . .'

'Mister Meehan!'

The youngster jumped like a stuck pig. '*Sir?*' he squealed.

One fleeting memory of the *Seepanther*'s captain. And the implacable warning in his expression as he'd said promisingly, 'If you deviate . . . I will be watching.'

'Order hard a port, Mister Meehan. Immediately, please.'

They understood instantly what it would mean. All of them did.

The boy sobbed with fright as Ainslie shouted, 'DON'T!' and then swung to face me. 'What the *hell* . . . ?'

'If we can lure him out then we've a chance of stopping him for good,' I broke across his protest. 'How many sinking ships, how many more dead men can you stand on *your* conscience, Mister Ainslie . . . ?'

The engines throbbed, and the broken funnel puttered raucously, and the Red Ensign flew stiff in the breeze which came from over that distant horizon.

Until . . .

'Aye, aye, Sir,' the young Third Mate said. Very softly.

The master of the already lost *Wellington Court* laid a gentle hand on the apprentice's shoulder. 'Thee heard what the captain said, lad,' Trueman murmured. 'The order was "Hard to port the wheel." '

And ever so gradually at first, then faster and faster, the bows of the *Maya Star* began to swing. I nodded through the darkness towards the strangely silent Able Seaman Cleese.

'Ask Mister Nolan for emergency full ahead. Now.'

And then I stepped to the after end of the bridge once again. It was surprisingly easy to find a strength in my voice, now the decision had been irrevocably taken.

'*Gun's* crew . . . Open *FIII*IIRE!'

Timmer's reaction was instantaneous. The joyful unquestioning battle cry of the born warrior.

'*Füüiiiire* . . .!'

Slam!

The first round screeching away into the night with the muzzle flash reflecting from every paralysed, disbelieving face on the lower decks.

Somebody, I never knew who it was and I hoped I never would, suddenly roared in a voice so full of hatred and unforgiveness, 'Oh you *bastard*, Barton . . . You've sold us out, ye lousy stinkin' basTAAAARD!'

'Wheel's hard a *port*, Sir,' the Bosun's threatening bellow swamping and battering into submission the accusing scream from aft.

And then Timmer's shell exploding ashore, over to the right of the barely decipherable German warship. Only a small, insignificant burst, hardly a miniscule flash against the vastness of that silent black jungle. Impotent, like the *Maya Star* herself.

'Train LEFT . . . On . . . On . . . ON . . .'

'Clear the bridge,' I snapped tightly. 'You've a chance of finding cover on the port side, all of you. I'll con the ship!'

'Go to hell. *Sir!*' Ainslie muttered nervously while all Cleese managed was a sickly grin and a dazed shake of the head. Trueman glanced at me and there was a rueful note in his voice.

'Happen it's academic, Mister. But can thee log a full cap'n for mutiny when he's not even signed on articles?'

'We'll argue it lat . . .' I'd started to retort. Then Ainslie blurted, 'Oh God, but she's moving again. She's coming *out*, Sir . . .'

'FIIIiiire!'

Slam!

'REload . . !'

'Any moment now,' little Meehan whispered, staring astern hypnotically. Cleese suddenly jumped. 'Second Engineer on the phone. Wants to know what the . . . what's happening up here.'

I grabbed it. 'Archie?'

The roar of the flat-out diesels almost drowned the distant voice this time. 'You started a war or what, chum?'

'Jus' remember your orders, Archie . . .' I stopped abruptly, every muscle in my back knotted against what I knew had to come in the next few seconds. 'In fact, get out now! Leave the throttles wide open an' get the hell up on deck. Keep to the port side . . .'

'CHRIST but it's comi . . .' Ainslie's numbed shout. Only I didn't need the warning, I'd already seen the speckle of flashes from the shore out of the corner of my eye – and that, in its turn, reminded me of the uninjured hostages below.

'Cut the Jerries loose an' bring 'em topside with you, Archie . . .' then the first promise of the *Seepanther*'s rage arrived on a shriek of displaced violence.

'DOWN!' someone was pleading desperately. 'Oh Holy Mary Mother o' Jes . . .'

The incoming sigh stopped. Dead! And then came the roar, and the clang of some great fist striking the hull. I clung rigidly to the rail as the ship began to lean over, shying to port while the sea along our starboard side sucked into a gigantic waterspout forest, white-rushing mushrooms of hissing spray towering high above the bridge itself, blanking out the stars and hovering for what seemed a very long time but could only have lasted for half the blink of a fear-glazed eye before collapsing back into the welter of sand-clouded foam already curling astern.

'*Christ*mas!' Cleese muttered a little obscurely.

'Short,' Captain Trueman said objectively, perhaps just a shade too tightly, as the *Maya Star* fought back to an even keel. Shaking the spray from my eyes I swung towards Meehan. The boy's expectant gaze was already on me, the phone to the poop still gripped firmly in his grimy hand.

'Starboard!' I snapped urgently. 'Hard a st'bd the wheel, son.'

'They aren't goin' to cease firing, you know. Not now,' the Third Mate pointed out with just the slightest hint of reproach. I shrugged and tried to offer a reassuring grin. It sort of got stuck half way and ended as a sickly comical grimace.

'Steering for the last fall of shot. Throws their gunners' ranging out . . .' I trailed off weakly, realizing they were all eyeing me with blank expressions. 'I . . . er . . . read it in a book once,' I finished defiantly. Then started to dive for the deck as I discovered that *Korvettenkapitän* Neugard must have borrowed his books from a different bloody library.

The flashes were the most appalling feature of those next horror-filled seconds. The white, searing flashes which seemed to throw every facet of the *Maya Star*'s superstructure into bleached relief so that even when I screwed my eyes tightly shut I still couldn't escape the nightmare realization that somebody, somewhere, was being cremated all because I wanted to be a bloody fighting sailorman. I knew that much, you see, because I could hear them on the deck below the bridge, screaming and whimpering as the white light overtook them and crisped them into stumbling, smoking things which still moved blindly from the engine room exit to the long drop over the missing shell-obliterated guard rails.

Dimly I was aware of my voice protesting in a disembodied sort of way, 'I told him . . . I *told* the Second Engineer to come out PORT side an' under cover, didn't I . . . ? Well, *didn't* I then f'r . . . ?'

Then Trueman was shaking me violently, dragging my fixed gaze away from the contorted and blackened section of deck where Archie Nolan and Greaser Hotchkiss and two German hostages had climbed straight from the cover of the

Maya Star's still-undamaged engine room into an exploding six-inch holocaust.

'Bring 'er ROUND, Mister, or she'll be hard aground like a . . .'

Noise, now. A bedlam of noise. The flames, the jetting roar of a fractured fire main, men shouting from aft above the clatter of running feet on steel plating . . .

'On target!'

'FIIIiiire!'

Slam!

'Midships the wheel . . . Starb'd twenty . . . Oh *Jesus!*'

'Sir? Please Sir, but I can't hear you, Sir . . .'

I found myself blinking stupidly at the white blob of little Meehan's face hovering above me. Even through the darkness and the drifting smoke I could see the bright blood running from his ears. 'You're all right. You'll be all right, son,' Ainslie was almost pleading.

'Get that bloody steering phone, somebody.'

I clawed myself erect, staring astern with liquid from the wound in my forehead trickling steadily through my brows. Wiping it clear savagely I struggled to make out the shape of the *Seepanther* again. Was she really under way, f'r God's sake? Was she really steaming down river now like Ainslie had claimed, or did Neugard simply intend to sit there and blow us apart without even vacating his safe little patch of South America. Because if he did . . .

Only I never quite finished speculating because that was the moment when the next salvo arrived without, for me at least, any warning. All I remember was a . . . a helter-skelter of explosions literally running and skipping towards me, all the way from the after end of the *Maya Star*, a racing, closing barrage of whining shrapnel and blackly-etched parts of ship silhouetted in stark flashes which seemed to portray to perfection all the agony and all the hopelessness of our futile, bloody awful war . . .

Timmer's gunners first, arching backwards now from the white light blossoming at the base of the gun in a monstrous

185

ballet of pain . . . Bosun Fletcher next, stolidly indestructible Bosun Fletcher captured in mid-blast as the scything splinters gutted both him and the *Wellington Court*'s Chief Officer in one disbelieving micro-second . . . young Second Wireless Operator Martin, even then dragging a fire hose along the deck towards us with dogged courage, until the *Seepanther*'s outrage outstripped him and spat a very large part of him clean through the rails and out into the black tropical sea . . .

'They've hit the saloon,' Ainslie was bawling hysterically into my ear. 'All those poor bastards in the saloon, Barton . . .'

'Get AFT, dammit!' I heard myself roaring back. 'Get aft an' take over the *wheel*, Mister . . .'

. . . but then there was a whole horde of screaming, bedlam gargantuans in the sky. Ear-piercing, homing . . . a king-sized carbon copy of an earlier, never-to-be-forgotten nightmare but even more difficult to bear this time because it hadn't been necess . . .

Somebody punching me in the belly with a sledge-hammer fist . . . the whole ship rearing and falling away as the world finally collapsed around me . . . more water, great avalanching slabs of water hanging white against the black sky while the glare of the explosions tearing us apart flickered and flashed across the stunned retina of my eye . . .

A voice was screaming above it all, a long horribly drawn-out plea for help and I went even colder than ever before when I recognized the source of that agonized and gradually fading hopelessness.

Even then I could hardly believe it. That a man like Bosun Fletcher could have been quite so frightened, and quite so anguished during the moments of what was perhaps his greatest victory – to be dying in the arms of a finally speechless ship's carpenter.

There was yet another ripple of fire from the dark jungle shore. I only had time to feel Ainslie crumple beside me with most of his right shoulder missing, and sob, 'I'm sorry . . . God *help* me but I'm SORRY, Three Oh . . .'

. . . when I realized that it wasn't another broadside from *Kapitän* Neugard's guns. Not this time.

But that it was the *Seepanther* blowing herself to pieces.

Just like I'd originally hoped she would. But that had been before the dying aboard the *Maya Star* had begun all over again . . .

EPILOGUE

I watched the enemy warship tear herself apart with a stunned, almost academic detachment, because my bruised and battered senses were really only able to share the agony and the anguish of my own ship and my own already ill-starred crew.

Even the initial indication of her destruction left me cold and numb . . . that first bright flash low down and squarely amidships against the *Seepanther*'s moving hull, illuminating the distant ship with a reflected brilliance and sending a million sparkling, flickering wavelets scurrying and racing towards us on the periphery of the blast.

A moment later came the second detonation – against her far side this time – while the whole cliff face behind her lit up with that same shocking white light, throwing the black silhouette of Neugard's doomed command into momentary macabre relief.

And then the explosions within. Great gouts of rolling fire gusting upwards as her ammunition compartments fused into one roaring, continuous chain of super-heated extinction . . . her masts caving inwards to span the inferno, her funnel whirling and flapping like an unrolling paper cylinder as it rose towards the night sky . . . her bridge deck and countless tons of superstructure lifting slowly up on top of the puffball, with *Korvettenkapitän* Neugard and *Kapitän-leutnant* Flindt and a whole flotilla of burned and blasted dead men still at their posts within that monstrously arcing sepulchre.

Until, just as suddenly, it was over. And the blackness descended as if it had never left that evil place, while the crackle of the rearing flames reached over and touched us across the sea and the only movement was in the slow drift of burning surface oil, the outgoing current already beginning to carry it away from the gutted hulk of the commerce raider *Seepanther* . . .

Eventually I dragged myself erect and stared dully over the decks of my own poor, tortured ship.

The gun's crew were still stumbling dazedly back to their posts. But Bombardier Timmer would never gaze through another gun sight, and never fire another round in gallant defiance. Those spectacles he'd so anxiously clung to had fractured under the force of the blasts which rocked the *Maya Star*, finally blowing inwards in a myriad of penetrating micro-shards.

Bombardier Timmer was blind.

Steward Thomson would never reach that hospital he had so bravely waited for, either. Steward Thomson was dead, blown to pieces as that shell impacted in the saloon on top of him and tough, resourceful Second Cook Gifford and the *Herr Doktor* and all the German wounded I hadn't had the heart to imprison down below.

It struck me then, in a sadly inconsequential way, that I'd never even learned the *Herr Doktor's* name . . .

Bosun Fletcher died agonizingly slowly from his horrific belly wound, and Chippie had never argued with him once, not all the time while he held him in his arms on that deck which had seen so many deaths. But I knew the old carpenter would look after Fletcher until the end. Until he tenderly inserted the very last stitch he would have to complete on this sad and hopeless voyage.

Third Mate Ainslie was dead, along with Sparks . . . Little Apprentice Meehan would never captain a ship of his own. Not now. Not unless they could find a way for a man to go to sea when his ear drums had been blasted into permanent silence, never to hear an order given or a ship's whistle sounding again . . .

But Cleese had lived through it. And Deckie Sullivan, and the indestructible Lamptrimmer with the bandage round his head and the light of battle still gleaming from his one visible eye. Captain Trueman, too, would sail another grey ship on another grey voyage to war . . .

While the *Maya Star* herself could reach a temporary haven even now. I learned that much as I braced myself to assess the damage from the devastating salvos which had straddled us. Because the fire had burnt itself out almost as quickly as it had begun, and by the grace of God our cargo remained unbreached while the ship still steamed doggedly as ever under the flag that not even a warship's rancour could destroy.

So eventually she would go home. But only after a long time, and with another crew, another company of men.

With only the memory of what had happened, and how it had happened, locked within her bones. About the way she had turned, just for one brief moment, on a vastly superior enemy. And beckoned. With a Judas hand.

Because we'd fought the *Seepanther* with lifeboats, in the end.

And I knew my Devil would have enjoyed that exquisite irony, that I had used a sailor's means of preserving life to destroy the lives of sailors.

Two lifeboats, to be precise. Two lifeboats, thirty empty dried egg tins, forty fathoms of good manilla rope reinforced by field telephone wire – and that sluggish, hanging vapour from the jungle which obscured the black surface of our river during the darkest hours of the night.

But there had been one more essential ingredient needed for the delivery of that desperately-conceived weapon – the intention of *Korvettenkapitän* Neugard to violate even the basic honour of war, to break his pledge and continue to follow us out to sea, because the energy for her own destruction had to be provided by the *Seepanther* herself . . . Only Neugard had fooled me, Neugard had proved himself too scrupulous a man by his own standards, so I had been the one who had to break my pledge – to turn provocatively to port, away from the track along which we were to release our hostages.

Whereupon the waiting *Seepanther* had begun to move again, sliding through that black water under the outraged bite of her propellers, with the curt commands relaying to her gunners . . . '*Feurlaubnis* . . . Permission to open fire!'

Moving faster now, closing with the spot where the *Maya Star* had been anchored only a few minutes before . . .

'*Schnell, schnell . . . ! Achtung Geschützbedienung . . . FEUER!*'

Her first salvo roaring away into the night, descending upon her contemptible adversary with Wagnerian fury . . .

. . . but then the raider's forefoot slicing monstrously into the trap we'd prepared. The reinforced rope buoyed to lie across the river between the two lifeboats lightly moored on either side of the channel . . . drawing taut under the warship's forward momentum, dragging the boats along with her . . . and inward, scissoring hard against her steel flanks . . .

Two lifeboats finally converging against either side of the *Seepanther*'s hull. And each boat ringed with over a ton of high explosive, a rubbing strake formed out of one hundred six-inch naval shells, secured like the knives on Boadicea's chariot – projecting outwards . . .

And every one a live round. Fitted with an instant fusehead. Set to blow on impact . . .

Slowly I walked aft, picking my way blindly through the gutted, twisted labyrinth of the superstructure and past the charred maw of number five hold.

I never looked back towards that funeral pyre on the edge of a jungle. Sights like that weren't for me, they were for warriors to observe, and victors to relish. I never had been a fighting sailor at heart – my victories lay in making a safe harbour after a quiet and uneventful voyage, not searching out and killing my enemy. I was a merchant seaman, one of the hunted and not one of the hunters.

But perhaps none of us could hope to turn away from our

devils in a war, and run for ever simply because we sailed in ships designed for peace and not equipped for standing firm. Being unprovocative hadn't allowed Jeremy Prethero to live for one moment longer all those endless days ago, or young boy Davidson or Gulliver, or even Quartermaster Tennison of the doleful eye and the calm acceptance of his own destruction.

And so it was for legions of other men like them who would follow in the *Maya Star*'s sad wake that I had betrayed an honourable enemy, and killed him with deceit and not by force of arms.

I hoped that Bosun Fletcher would understand why he had died in that moment, too. And Thomson, and Chef Gifford and Third Mate Ainslie and all those others who had reached their ultimate harbour.

And if they couldn't understand, then I prayed that they would forgive.

Because my Devil wouldn't. I knew he would always be there waiting. And that no matter where I voyaged to for the rest of my life I would never find another deep, and truly blue, sea . . .